Grace
Stirs It Up

by Mary Casanova

★ American Girl®

For my niece, Grace, who shares the same lovely name

Questions or comments? Call 1-800-845-0005, visit **americangirl.com**, or write to Customer Service, American Girl, 8400 Fairway Place, Middleton, WI 53562-0497.

Printed in China
15 16 17 18 19 20 21 22 LEO 12 11 10 9 8 7 6 5 4 3 2 1

Illustrations by Sarah Davis

Author photo credit, p. 178: James Hanson

Special thanks to Héloïse Blain, French teacher and language expert, Nice, France; Dawn Bowlus, director, Jacobson Institute for Youth Entrepreneurship at The University of Iowa; Dominique Dury, head chef, Flying Cook, Paris, France; and Donna Houle, special projects manager, Blackstone Valley Tourism Council.

Cataloging-in-Publication Data available from the Library of Congress.

Contents

A Backyard Walk
Chapter 1

*G*race, darlin'!" Mom's singsongy voice drifted to my ears from somewhere nearby. "Someone *needs* you."

I forced one eye open, then the other, expecting to see my cousin's bedroom back in Paris.

But instead, on my sage-green rug, my suitcase waited to be unpacked. Beneath my print of two penguins with their heads entwined, my purple backpack hung on my desk chair. And from outside my screened window, a robin whistled brightly: *cheeriup, cheerio, cheeriup . . .*

"Grace," Mom called again from the bottom of the stairs.

I found my voice. "Okay, I'm coming."

I slid out of bed, still in my travel clothes. I'd left Paris at 8:30 this morning and hadn't slept a wink on the plane. After six hours of flying and an hour-long

drive from Boston, I'd arrived home only to find that
time had almost stood still. My bedroom clock had still
said 10:00 in the morning, but my body thought it was
late afternoon. It had felt so good to be home that I'd
flopped down on my bed and slept.

Now that I was waking up, I suddenly *remembered*,
and a surge of energy zipped through me. "Bonbon!"

I raced down the stairs and into the kitchen.

Mom was stirring a pitcher of lemonade. "Hi,
sleepyhead! You napped for almost two hours. Lunch
soon."

Whining rose from the dog crate near the back
door. I spun toward the little black nose pressed against
the wire door. Bonbon looked up at me with her sweet
black eyes, one framed by a pirate patch of dark fur.
At last, at last—here in Bentwick, Massachusetts—she
finally had a *real* home.

"You're really here," I said, opening the crate and
lifting her into my arms. She wiggled and squirmed
with energy.

"I think she needs to go out," Mom said.

I stepped into my flip-flops, grabbed the pink
leash that Mom had bought for Bonbon, and set the dog

on the kitchen floor. "Let's go, pup!"

Bonbon twisted and spun, but I managed to attach her leash to her new collar.

"I hope she's that excited for her vet appointment on Thursday," Mom said, laughing. "I called this after noon, and they can get her in for a quick checkup. And speaking of exciting news, Grandma and Grandpa invited us over for dinner tonight at six. They're anxious to see us."

"Can I bring Bonbon along?"

Mom shrugged. "Call and ask when you come back inside," she suggested. "See what they say."

I nodded and then stepped out the back door into a warm, humid day. Bonbon darted left and right. Nose to the ground, she snuffled, snorted, and sniffed every inch of grass in our backyard, straining at her leash.

Each time she pulled hard, I took a tiny dog treat from my pocket—just as Mom had suggested. Bonbon wasn't used to walking on a leash, so we had to teach her not to tug.

"Bonbon," I said sweetly. "Come."

She turned, spotted my outstretched hand, and trotted a few steps back toward me.

"Sit, Bonbon," I said firmly. When she did, I praised her, and then said, "Let's walk." I held the treat in front of her nose and started walking again. She stayed close to my side for a few steps, so I gave her the treat. "Good girl!"

And then we went back to exploring. Every time Bonbon strained, I repeated the treat lesson. I wished that I could let her run free in the yard, but there were gaps in the stone wall—gaps that Bonbon could easily escape through. So until Dad had a chance to put in gates, Bonbon would be exploring the yard on a leash.

I don't mind a little extra work, I thought, breathing in the sweet, earthy air. Though I had loved Paris and my time there with Mom, my cousin Sylvie, Uncle Bernard, Aunt Sophie, and their new baby, Lily, there was nothing like being home again.

Within our stone wall, Mom's flower gardens and rhubarb patch had survived our being gone. The hydrangea bush was a ball of blue blossoms. Roses and lilies bloomed in shades of red and yellow. Mom's metal sculpture creations—a three-foot gnome and a heron standing on one leg—peered out from the flowers, as if welcoming me back.

A Backyard Walk

Yesterday, Paris. Today, *home*. Flying happened so fast that my brain couldn't catch up.

Bonbon nudged my foot with her wet nose. I reached down and scratched her under her chin. "We're world travelers," I said to her.

I thought back to that first day in Paris when Sylvie and I had walked through the Luxembourg Gardens—the day that I'd first met Bonbon. Skittish and mistrustful, the little French bulldog had come close to us only because Sylvie had bread in her hand. Then I began setting food and water just outside my aunt and uncle's *pâtisserie*, and eventually Bonbon started showing up for dinner every day. When she didn't show up one day, I was heartsick, wondering what had happened to her.

To my huge surprise, Mom had found Bonbon through the animal shelter and adopted her, and we flew her back to the States with us. "Since you're the one who has been asking for a dog," Mom had said on the plane, "she'll be mostly your responsibility."

Okay with me!

I headed for the end of our yard, where ivy spiraled up the trunks of towering maples and oaks, their leafy tops like massive green umbrellas. From their branches hung about a dozen birdhouses that Dad had made in every size, shape, and color.

A gray squirrel swung from the blue, double-decker birdhouse. Head down, tail flicking angrily, it chattered and scolded us.

In return, Bonbon yipped, barked, and bolted for the tree.

"Bonbon, no!" I held on to her leash with both hands. But Bonbon pulled forward, and I tripped over my flip-flops and fell flat on my chest, my arms outstretched. "*Oomph!*"

As I lay there, the squirrel disappeared into the neighbor's yard. Bonbon stopped barking. She must have sensed that something had gone wrong. She wheeled around, whined, and licked my cheek.

I laughed. "That didn't go so well, did it?" I rose to my feet and brushed fresh grass clippings off my clothes. "Are you going to be a troublemaker?"

In answer, Bonbon spun in an excited circle.

Then I picked her up and let her look over the ledge of the stone wall. "Want to see?"

Between our house and the Blackstone River beyond, mallards dipped and bobbed in the canal. "See that towpath alongside the canal?" I said to Bonbon. "It used to be where horses pulled barges loaded with cargo from the mills. You would have loved racing after those horses, wouldn't you?"

Her ears stood up nice and straight, as if she was really listening, so I continued.

"See, some parts of the river are too shallow to get through, so a long time ago, they made the canal," I explained. "But now, you and I can use those towpaths for walking."

Bonbon wiggled, as if bored, but I held her more tightly so that she wouldn't fall. To our right, a bike rider approached on the path.

"And you see that silver-and-orange bike coming this way? That boy riding it is my brother, Josh."

Josh spotted us and waved as he crossed the nearest small bridge to our side of the canal. Though Dad and Josh had picked us up from the airport, we still had so much catching up to do.

I put Bonbon down, and then we dashed around the side of the house and met Josh on the driveway.

"Hi!" I said as he rolled his bike into the garage.

"Hey, sis," he said, tossing his head to send his

bangs out of his eyes. "Thought you were going to sleep all day."

"She almost did," Dad said, looking up from his workbench in the garage. "But if you need sleep, you need sleep. Right, Grace?"

"Yeah, especially if my body thinks it's six hours later than it really is." I smothered a yawn.

Josh said, "Y'know, studies show teens really do need more sleep to be at their best. So at fourteen, I should probably be sleeping till noon on weekends, don't you think?"

"Seems you're at your best, Josh, when you're busy," Dad said. "Sleep may not have that much to do with it."

Josh grinned. "Yeah. True." As if to prove the point, he reached for a wrench, which meant he was about to start tinkering with his bike.

I led Bonbon through the garage door back into the kitchen, suddenly remembering that I needed to call Grandma. I couldn't wait for her to meet Bonbon!

A Revolutionary Idea
Chapter 2

When late afternoon rolled around, Josh biked off ahead of us to Grandma and Grandpa's house. With Mom and Dad just behind me, I walked Bonbon on a leash along the towpath into the heart of town. I had a pocketful of treats and gave one to Bonbon every so often to try to keep her by my side.

To our left, the evening sun turned the Blackstone into a flowing river of gold. It was a different kind of gilding than at the Palace of Versailles, which I had visited in France just a few days ago, but our river town had a beauty all its own.

When we reached First Street, we turned right and headed uphill. Bonbon stopped to sniff at every lamp-post and flower garden, but I didn't mind. Everything was new to her here, and thankfully, she was no longer roaming the streets of Paris looking for something to eat and somewhere to sleep.

We passed a few shops and restaurants, including Da Vinci's, my favorite Italian restaurant. At the next corner, we all glanced through the window of First Street Family Bakery, my grandparents' bakery business. The sign in the dark window read "Closed," as it always did by late afternoon.

At the end of the block, we crossed the railroad tracks near the depot. A crowd of tourists waited to board the restored diesel train, used for sightseeing trips through Blackstone Valley.

To think only yesterday, I was a tourist, too—in Paris.

It felt strange to be back home only to have my best friends, Ella and Maddy, *gone*. We'd been in touch online when I was in Paris, but now they were at Maddy's family cabin in the Berkshires, the mountains in western Massachusetts.

Mom seemed to read my mind. As we passed the public library, housed in an old steeple-topped white church, she asked, "When do your friends get back, Grace?"

I glanced over my shoulder. She and Dad followed

behind me, holding hands. I guess they'd missed each other, too.

"Late tonight," I replied. "I can't *wait* to show them Bonbon. We're going to meet up tomorrow afternoon, I think."

Bonbon's ears perked up at the sound of her name, and she trotted a little faster up the hill. Houses stood shoulder to shoulder here, a few dating back over two hundred years to the time of the American Industrial Revolution. Others were brand-new, but you could hardly tell. They had the same wooden shutters and cobblestone walkways.

At last, we reached the familiar brick house with dormers and cranberry trim. Grandma was waiting for us on the landing, and she wrapped me up in a hug.

"Oh, your little dog! Grace, she's almost as cute as you!" Grandma reached down to pet Bonbon, but my dog backed away to the end of her leash.

"She's shy at first," I explained. "It takes her a little time to warm up to people."

"That's fine," Grandma said, opening the door wide. "Sometimes I'm slow to warm up to people, too."

In the pale blue living room with cherry furniture

and an Oriental rug, Grandpa popped up from his easy chair, set his book on the coffee table, and greeted me and Mom. "Welcome home, girls!"

I smiled. I guess even though she's a fifth-grade teacher, Mom will always be his "girl."

"So how do people greet each other in *Par-ee*?" Grandpa asked.

I thought of the first day I'd stepped into the apartment in Paris, a little bewildered by the kissing-on-each-cheek thing. And I'd bonked Sylvie's nose, which hadn't been the best way to get to know each other.

Grandpa had done lots of traveling when he served in the navy, so I guessed he already knew the answer to his question, but I explained anyway. "People in France kiss on the cheek, both sides, but only if you're a close friend or family. Otherwise, you just shake hands."

"So how do I rank, Grace?" Grandpa asked.

I stood on my tiptoes, breathed in his smell of spice and soap, and kissed him on each cheek.

"Phew!" he said, with mock relief. "I guess I'm family."

Then Mom gave him a hug. "Hey, Dad," she said. "It's so good to see you!"

Soon we were all sitting in the small backyard, overlooking the river below. The picnic table was covered with dishes of green beans, cucumbers, corn on the cob, fruit salad, and barbecued chicken hot off the grill.

Grandma and Grandpa filled us in on what Mom and I had missed while we were away: a runaway horse at the Fourth of July parade, the closing of a gift shop on Main Street, and the opening of a big shoe store at the mall.

Mom and I answered questions about our trip, but no words could come close to summing it up.

"We loved our visit to Versailles," Mom said.

"We did!" I added. "That's where an angry mob stormed the palace at the start of the French Revolution."

Grandpa leaned in. "That was a very different kind of revolution from what happened right here in Blackstone Valley," he said. "The American Industrial Revolution."

I'd heard Grandpa give this talk before, so I knew what was coming.

"The Slater Mill in Blackstone Valley was the first

water-powered cotton-spinning factory in the whole United States," Grandpa began, settling back into his chair. "Before that, farmwork started and stopped with the rising and setting of the sun. But with that first factory, workers were governed by the factory bell. It was all about speed and efficiency. And after the Slater Mill was built, more and more mills sprang up here in New England."

Even if Grandpa had told us this story eighty million times already, I didn't mind.

I jumped, though, when a whistle sounded and the sightseeing train started chugging in our direction, pulling six train cars. We all watched and waited for the train to pass.

From behind the windows of the dining car, tourists young and old waved at us. We waved back as the train crossed the narrow tracks high above the river below.

"'Course," Grandpa continued with a nod at the passing train, "with the Industrial Revolution came the need for transportation. Before trains came along, they needed to move heavy cargo between the mills and the port by boat. But they couldn't get large boats down the river."

"So is that why they built the canal and towpaths?" Josh asked, playing along. I knew that Josh already knew the answer—he was just humoring Grandpa.

But Grandpa took the bait. He nodded. "That's right. In the early eighteen hundreds, they built the Blackstone Canal. Did you know that a barge on that canal could haul up to thirty-five tons of cargo pulled along the towpath by only two horses?"

"Hmm . . . I'd heard that somewhere," said Dad, scratching his chin.

Mom shot him a look.

"But the barges were slow," Grandpa continued. "And *that's* why trains were so revolutionary."

Before he could get too far on the history of trains, Mom spoke up. "By the way, Grace has come up with a pretty revolutionary idea of her own."

"Oh, let's hear!" Grandma met my eyes and lifted her red glasses to the top of her gray hair, as if to see me better. But I knew the real reason was that her bifocals—no matter how stylish—sometimes gave her trouble.

Despite my feeling tired, a tiny spark of energy

ignited within me. "Well, all summer I've been thinking about starting a business with my friends. Since
I love baking, I kept coming back to that idea. But
to make it stand out and be really unique, I finally
thought, why not give it a French twist?"

"Wonderful," Grandma said.

Grandpa nodded his approval, too. "It's always
good to try and look at things differently."

It felt so good to be together again with family, but
now that I was talking about starting a business with
my friends, I needed to see *them*, too. Why did Ella and
Maddy have to be away when I was finally back?
I rested my chin on my folded arms.

The three of us had had a blast together last summer. A whole week at Lake Liberty in the Berkshires. A
whole week of swimming, kayaking, and sleeping on
the screened porch. And I'd missed it this year.

While I was away, I'd tried to keep in touch with
my friends through my travel blog, and I *hoped, hoped,
hoped* that things hadn't changed between us. It was
August fourth. We still had almost a month of vacation
left, and I was excited to pick up where we'd left off.
Now that Ella and Maddy had given up on their dog-

walking business, I couldn't wait to tell them about my great idea for a French baking business we could start together!

But what if they didn't like it?

"Grace, you're drooping," Dad said.

Startled out of my thoughts, I looked up. "Huh?"

"You look like a plant that needs water," Grandma said. "Or a girl who needs sleep."

"Jet lag," Mom said. "It's catching up with me, too." She glanced at her watch. "It's only seven thirty," she said, "but my body thinks it's one thirty in the morning. Way past my bedtime." She yawned. "What about you, Grace?"

Yawning is contagious.

I yawned long and slow in reply. "I'm ready for bed, and . . ." I tilted my head under the picnic table. In the shadows, Bonbon rested her head on my feet, and from her little black nose came soft, muffled breathing. "And so is Bonbon. She's snoring."

Mom smiled at Dad. "Honey, isn't that sweet? Now you're not the only one in the family who snores."

I giggled as Dad made a face at Mom.

"How about I give you world travelers a lift home?"

Grandpa said.

We lived only a mile and a half away, but I wasn't about to argue.

The Name Game
Chapter 3

*T*he next morning, before I could even open the back door, Bonbon piddled on the kitchen floor. "Bonbon, no," I said firmly. "You have to learn how to hold it."

Crating her was supposed to help prevent accidents, but—my goodness—she had to use a *little* self-control between the crate and the backyard.

I sighed. As part of her training, I took her outside right away, just to help her understand how things are supposed to work.

Then we came back inside and I used a wet rag to clean up the mess.

Cleaning up after a dog wasn't my idea of a great way to start a morning, but it came with owning a dog. Or at least *this* dog.

Bonbon looked up at me with her puppy dog eyes

while I worked, and my frustration melted away. "Don't worry, Bonbon," I said. "You're worth it."

After breakfast, I took Bonbon for a walk along the towpath (with a plastic dog-waste bag, of course). Then I joined Mom on the couch. Bonbon curled up between us as I turned on my tablet.

"How's it going?" Mom asked.

"We're working on it," I replied, scratching Bonbon under the chin. She licked my hand.

With my feet on the embroidered footstool, I sat across from the empty fireplace and checked my online calendar. I added "walk Bonbon" to my late afternoon schedule. With her energy, one long walk a day didn't seem to be enough.

"You're so organized," Mom said, glancing over from her spiral notebook of lesson plans.

"Thanks," I said.

"*Scary* organized," Josh said, heading from the kitchen to the upright piano on the other side of the room.

"Scary?" I asked.

"What nine-year-old keeps a calendar?" he said, sitting at the piano, his back turned to me.

"Scary," Mom said, "is what I'd call your *room*, Josh. You were practically growing science projects in there while we were away. Good thing I returned to do an inspection before it was too late."

Josh's bedroom always looks as if a hurricane had swept through it. Yesterday, Mom came out of his room with a half-finished chocolate shake growing a mound of fuzzy mold.

"Two questions, Josh," I said, teasing. "First, who wouldn't finish a chocolate shake? And second, how can you even *think* when your room's so messy?"

Josh ignored me at first. He started to plunk out a one-handed melody, and then added chords. Then he said over his shoulder, "How can you sleep with your room so crazy neat and organized?"

Pretending to be insulted, I said, "I . . . sleep . . . just . . . fine."

Though Josh had never wanted to take piano lessons, he had a way of learning on his own. He'd taught himself chords, and his fingers flew over the keys, playing music he'd heard or coming up with his own melodies.

I was on my second year of piano lessons, but

playing the piano didn't come as naturally to me as
it did for my big brother.

"Hey, Josh?" I said.

"Yeah?"

"That sounds nice."

"Yeah?"

"Yeah."

Then I turned back to my calendar.

Wednesday, August 5th

12:00	*Video-chat with Sylvie*
1:00	*Practice piano*
3:00	*Meet at Ella's house—walk Bonbon and Murphy*

Murphy was Ella's dog, and I was pretty sure that
Bonbon would have a good time playing with him.
Only four and a half more hours until we met up!

"Mom," I said, "I can't wait to share my idea with
Ella and Maddy about a baking business."

"Sounds like fun," she said, but I could tell that
her mind was somewhere else. She still wasn't totally
on board with my plan. Every time I had tried to tell
her about the baking business, she sort of tuned out—

as if she imagined that I'd spend an hour with my
friends in the kitchen and then move on to my next
big idea.

But this time—this *idea*—felt different. I carried it
around with me. I went to bed thinking about it. I woke
up thinking about it.

I glanced at my calendar. There was still time in my
day to try something new.

"Mom, before we call Sylvie and Aunt Sophie, do
you mind if I bake some cookies?"

"Sure," she said. "Let me know if you need help. But
the better you get at baking," she said, patting her belly,
"the more miles I have to run. The half marathon is just
a month away. And with the news I got this morning,
I'm feeling a little overwhelmed."

"What news?"

She made a face that looked like a plea for help.
"That I'll be teaching fourth grade instead of fifth this
year."

"Really? That's great! Will I be in your class?"
I asked.

"No, I don't think it's a good idea for you and
me to be in the same classroom. Nothing personal,"

she said, smiling.

"Nothing personal? Mom, but this *is* personal. Why can't I be in your class?"

"Okay, let me rephrase: because it is personal. Because you and I are mother and daughter. I think our close relationship would get in the way for me, and probably for you, too."

I was about to protest, but Mom touched my cheek lightly. "Sweetheart. You'll have to trust me on this. You'll do fine with any of the other teachers. But for me, what this change means is that I'll have to come up with a whole new set of lesson plans—and it's already August." She shook her head. "I'll be lucky if I find time to breathe before school starts up, let alone be ready for the half marathon at the end of the month. Maybe I should just let it go this year."

I sat straight up. "Mom, no way. You've been working too hard. You even ran most of the time in Paris. You can do it!"

She shrugged. "I don't know. I'm just a little stressed right now."

As Mom turned back to her lesson plans and Josh's piano music filled the living room, I set down my tablet

and hopped up from the couch. Bonbon woke up and
followed me into the kitchen. Immediately, she started
circling on the hardwood floor by the door, a signal
that she had to go out. *Again.*

I didn't get it. I'd just taken Bonbon for a walk, but
maybe the change in time between Paris and here was
throwing her off, too.

"Okay, okay," I said. "Hang on." But before I could
even get my flip-flops on to take her outside, Bonbon
squatted and left a yellow puddle.

"No!" But it was too late.

"What is it?" Mom called.

I took a deep breath. "I've got it under control,
Mom. Bonbon had another accident."

I sighed, and once again took her outside to show
her where I wanted her to go. And then when we came
back in, I cleaned up her mess. Again.

Taking care of a little dog that was used to living
on the streets was a lot harder than I'd thought it would
be. But I *had* to make this work. I was already too in
love with Bonbon to imagine not having her here
with me.

When I finished cleaning up, I took Bonbon outside

again and walked her around the yard.

"Maybe it's hard for you to adjust to life in the States the same way I had a tough time getting used to Paris at first," I thought out loud. "Change isn't easy, is it, girl?"

Bonbon whined a little at me and then tugged at her leash.

"You'll get used to things," I reassured her, following close behind. "Eventually."

After I finished baking a batch of gingersnap cookies, I went online with Mom to video-chat with Sylvie and her family in Paris.

With her sandy hair in a side-swept ponytail, Sylvie appeared on my tablet screen, holding Napoléon, her golden tabby cat, up next to her face.

"*Meeeeow,*" Napoléon complained, and then wiggled out of her arms and bolted out of view.

"Napoléon, *le chat,*" I said, practicing a little French.

"Where is Bonbon, the *dog*?" Sylvie asked, her smile as big as her eyes.

The Name Game

When I'd first arrived in Paris, I'd misunderstood Sylvie's shyness. I'd thought maybe she didn't want me sharing her bedroom for half the summer. But I'd learned she was just as uncomfortable as I was trying to communicate in a different language.

Now, even though we still had so much to learn with English and French, I felt closer to Sylvie than ever. I just wished she wasn't so many, many miles away. At least through video-chatting, we could see each other, even if we couldn't always find the right words to say what we wanted to say.

I pulled Bonbon closer to my side so that Sylvie could see her. *"Voilà!"* I said. "Here she is!"

"Bonjour, Bonbon!" Sylvie said. She added a bunch of words in French that I didn't understand, but her smile told me what I needed to know. She was clearly happy to see her little friend, and happy to know that the dog had a forever home.

"Bonbon misses you," I said. "And I miss you, too, Sylvie!"

But Bonbon wriggled this way and that, trying to escape. The more tightly I held on, the more she slipped like a bar of soap, right out from under my arm. She dropped to the floor with a *thud*.

"Oh no," I said, reaching down for her. "Bonbon, are you okay?" But she bolted away from me and out of the room.

When I glanced back at the screen, Aunt Sophie appeared with Baby Lily (short for Lilou in French) in her arms.

"Hi! How are you feeling, sis?" Mom asked her.

Unlike the tired Aunt Sophie I remembered from the days after Lily was first born, now Aunt Sophie almost glowed. "My energy is starting to come back. But that doesn't mean I'm going to start training for a half marathon. Yours is coming up, isn't it?"

Mom nodded. "I'm a long way yet from feeling ready."

"You'll do great," said Aunt Sophie. "Hey, Grace, how's Bonbon?"

"She's super sweet," I said. "But she ran off. I don't think she likes video-chatting that much."

My aunt smiled back. "Tell me, how is your new business idea coming along?"

"It's not very far along yet," I said, "but I'm telling my friends all about it this afternoon."

⟡ The Name Game ⟡

Then Sylvie leaned in and asked something in French. My aunt translated and said, "Sylvie wishes you lived closer so she could help."

Sylvie beamed at me.

"*Moi aussi*, Sylvie! I wish we lived closer, too. And I would love your help!"

What I wished I could tell her was that she *already* helped me, every time I saw her face on my tablet screen. Remembering the fun we'd had together in *La Pâtisserie* made me that much more excited about starting my baking business!

⟡

Before I met up with my friends, I found a black-and-white polka-dot ribbon in Mom's sewing supplies. I made a little bow with it and tied it onto Bonbon's collar. We were ready! Before heading out, I snapped a photo. *Click!*

Bonbon snuffled and sniffed her way without any problems for seven blocks. But the moment we walked up Ella's driveway toward her green house with overflowing flower boxes, my well-behaved little dog turned into a *wild* dog. Bonbon's yipping and yapping turned as shrill as nails on a blackboard as she strained at the end of her leash.

"No, Bonbon. Settle down," I said. "No barking!" Quickly, I reached into my pocket for a dog treat, but she didn't see it.

Her whole body was fixated on Murphy—the shaggy gray dog that was twice her size. At the other end of Murphy's leash, Ella hung on as her dog bounded toward us, pulling Ella behind in her shorts and tennis shoes. She looked taller and her copper-brown legs looked longer than at the start of the summer.

"Mur-phy!" she scolded, flipping her long black braid over her shoulder.

Trailing after them was Maddy, her wavy red hair kissed with sun and her face, arms, and legs sporting more freckles than I remembered.

"Hi, Maddy! Hi, Ella!" I shouted above the ruckus. "This is Bonbon!"

When we let the dogs get close enough to sniff noses, Bonbon stopped yipping. I was ready to pull back on her leash if either dog started acting mean. But as I squatted down, Bonbon finally caught sight—or scent—of the treat I held in my hand.

She sat down and looked up at me.

"Good dog," I said, and offered her the treat.

Murphy caught on fast. He sat down, too. And I gave him a treat, as well.

Seconds later, the treats were already forgotten and the dogs were yipping at each other again. Their backs turned into hairbrushes—bristles up! Uh-oh.

But I soon saw that along with the growling and whining, Bonbon was wagging her tail, too.

"She's confused," I said, and then joked, "Maybe dogs speak a different language in Paris?"

Ella laughed.

Murphy started wagging his tail, too—a good sign—as the two dogs began to circle and sniff, circle and sniff.

Bonbon lowered her head to her paws, her little rump in the air, tail keeping time.

"I think she wants to play," I said.

"Let's take them into the backyard instead of walking them," Ella suggested. "That way they can play—and work on their dog languages."

Ella's backyard was framed by a tall wooden

fence, perfect for a doggy playdate. Soon Bonbon and Murphy were taking turns chasing each other around the swing set, sandbox, and tire swing.

The backyard was usually occupied by one or all of Ella's three-year-old brothers—a set of *triplets*. But as we settled into red Adirondack chairs, Ella explained that they were all inside napping. "My mom decided to do the same," she said with a grin.

I nearly bounced on the edge of my chair, eager to share my new business idea with my friends. But first I had to answer all their questions about Bonbon. And listen as they told me about wakeboarding on Lake Liberty.

Ella giggled. "You should have seen Maddy's wipeout!"

"*My* wipeout? What about your face-plant?" Maddy replied with a laugh.

"I was just trying to avoid those ducklings!" Ella said.

"You wakeboarded, too, Ella?" I asked. She'd never been brave enough to try it in the past.

"Uh, no." She dropped her gaze to the grass, and then looked up again. "I was going to jump off the end of the dock. Then just as I pushed off, a bunch of little mallards shot out from under the dock. I thought I was going to land on them, so I did—"

Maddy interrupted. "She did what is now known as the famous Ella Twist."

Ella nodded. "To avoid them, I did a giant bellyflop instead."

"Awesome!" Maddy said, and they both started giggling again.

I smiled, but I felt completely left out. They'd had five weeks of fun without me. They'd shared laughs and moments over the summer that I would never know about.

I tried to close what felt like a widening gap between us. "Hey, you know how we talked about starting a business before I left in June?" I began.

"Yeah," Maddy said. "And now school's only a month away! I can't believe it. My mom's already got our back-to-school shopping all planned out. Maybe you two can join us!"

"I still can't wait to find out who we have for teachers," Ella said.

I wanted to get back to talking about my business

idea, but first I shared Mom's news about teaching fourth grade.

"Maybe we'll all be in her class!" Maddy said right away.

"You two might be, but I won't," I said, my mood dampening. "My mom said moms and daughters are 'too close' to be in the same classroom—that it gets too personal."

Bonbon suddenly squeezed under my chair to escape Murphy, and then stretched out to rest. Murphy flopped on the grass beside Ella, panting. Ella laughed and reached down to scratch Murphy's belly.

Before the conversation could get away from me again, I said, "Maddy, Ella, *listen* to me"—a little louder than I'd intended. "I have a business idea I really want to tell you about."

A look crossed between them, making me wonder if they'd completely cooled off on starting a business together. Neither said a word, so I jumped in. I had to!

I told them about how much fun it had been working in the *pâtisserie*. I told them how I'd looked around me the whole time I was in Paris, trying to find business ideas.

"What I didn't realize until just before I flew home was that the idea was right in front of me," I explained. "My grandpa gave me advice: 'Do what you love. And make it unique.' So I thought, I love baking, and to make a baking business more unique, we could bake French treats!"

Ella chewed her lip, the way she did when she was thinking hard.

"French treats?" said Maddy.

I nodded.

She tilted her head of copper-red hair. "But this is Massachusetts, Grace. You're back in the U-S-A. Do you think anyone really *wants* French treats?"

Maddy's words stung, taking me by surprise. Maybe she was jealous about my trip to Paris. I really didn't know, but either way, I pushed ahead.

"Wait till you see what I learned to make, Maddy. They're like pieces of art," I said. "It's like making art you can eat." I smiled, trying to convince my friends.

"Hmm," Maddy said. I could tell she was warming up. "I like the artsy part of it."

Ella was still silent, but she was thinking hard, I could tell. So I kept going. "We'd have a lot of fun together, and we could bake things that are really unique."

Maddy slowly nodded. "We'll have to buy supplies," she said, "but I have some money saved up."

At that, Ella's forehead wrinkled, her lower lip quivered, and tears suddenly fell.

"What's wrong, Ella?" I asked. "Is my idea that bad?"

Ella shook her head and took in a shaky breath. "No, it has nothing to do with your idea. I've been wanting to tell you two, but I was waiting for the right time. Now that you're back, Grace . . ."

"What?" Maddy and I said at the same time.

Ella wiped away tears, and she exhaled sharply. "My dad . . . lost his job."

My stomach clenched. I couldn't imagine if either of my parents lost their jobs. I knew they both needed to work to pay our bills.

"When?" I asked Ella, not knowing what else to say.

"In June, right after school got out. He's been looking for work ever since. So Maddy," Ella said, looking at the ground, "I know you want to go school shopping together, but . . . I just can't go with you."

"Oh," Maddy said. "You could still—"

Ella shook her head, and then sat up straighter. She looked at Maddy and then at me. "It would be great to start a business and make some money, because then I could buy my own supplies and clothes for school. But right now, I have to say no. I don't have the money to buy supplies to get started."

A silence settled over us. Then I had an idea.

"Ella," I said, jumping up from my chair, "what if you helped out the business in other ways at first? And then if we make money, you could pay us back later for supplies."

"Really?" Ella said, a smile spreading slowly across her face.

Maddy and I looked at each other and nodded.

Ella looked relieved, but also a little embarrassed. So I quickly changed the subject. "What should we call our business?"

"Got it!" Maddy said, extending her arms. "How about 'Bakers Three'?"

"Or 'Friends Three,'" Ella piped up. "I mean, because we are really good friends."

I smiled at Ella. "I like that. But maybe it should

sound more French," I suggested.

Maddy jumped up from her chair, interrupting me. "I know. I've got it! 'Ella, Maddy, and Grace's Little French Bakery'!"

I nodded. "That's good because it tells customers what we're selling," I said, "but it's a little long. In France, instead of bakeries, there are *boulangeries* and *pâtisseries*. What if we call our business *'La Pâtisserie'*?"

"Hmm," Maddy said. "It needs something more."

As Ella knelt down to adjust the bow on Bonbon's collar, she laughed. "I know! How about 'Perfectly Precious Polka-Dot Pâtisserie'?"

"Lots of 'p' sounds," Maddy said. "I like it! What's that called again?"

"It's called 'alliteration,'" I said, realizing I sounded like a teacher's daughter. "I like the sound of it, too. But the name's still a little too long. I mean, try saying that three times really fast!"

We all tried until we tripped over our twisted, tangled tongues. I plopped down into the grass, laughing, which alarmed Bonbon, who immediately jumped up to lick my face.

"Don't worry, *petite chienne*," I said, which meant

"little dog" in French. It was what I'd called Bonbon before I had finally given my furry friend a name.

Then I sat up. "That's it! How about *'La Petite Pâtisserie'*? It means 'little bakery.' Isn't that perfectly precious?" I glanced at my friends' faces, and I could tell they agreed. We had a name!

Before bed, I checked my e-mail and found a message from Sylvie. She had attached a photo of Napoléon, stretched out like a golden lion at the foot of her bed.

She wrote: *Mon chat dort sur mon lit.*

I tried to translate it and wrote back in English: "My cat sleeps on my bed. Yes?"

Then I sent off an e-mail about my day, including the photo of Bonbon with her bow. With a little help from my French dictionary, I added the French words for "My little dog is very fashionable": *Ma petite chienne est très à la mode.*

À la mode? I giggled. In America, *à la mode* also means "with ice cream." I pictured Bonbon with a scoop of ice cream on her head. Of course, she'd think that was a fine idea. Let it melt, and—*voilà!*—she'd take care of the mess.

Then I wrote more in English, telling Sylvie how Bonbon's fashionable bow had, in a way, helped my friends and me come up with the name of our business. Funny how one good idea can lead to the next . . .

The Great Escape
Chapter 4

hen Ella and Maddy arrived at my back door for our first morning of baking, Bonbon greeted them with twirls, wags, and kisses. When Maddy tripped over her, I decided it was safer for everyone for Bonbon to go back in her crate while we worked. She whined at first, but then settled in for her morning nap.

As I stood up, I smoothed out my new apron, which was black with pink polka dots and a satiny pink ribbon.

"Hey, that's adorable!" Maddy said as I turned around to model the apron for my friends.

"It's my going-away gift from Colette, who worked at my aunt and uncle's *pâtisserie*," I explained. "She made one for Sylvie, too, almost identical."

"I didn't even think to bring an apron," Maddy said.

"I mean, not that I have one."

"Me neither," said Ella, glancing down at her sundress.

"That's okay," I said quickly, and then I thought of a solution: "There are a *bunch* of aprons at my grandparents' bakery. I'll bring some next time we meet. That way you can choose your own!"

Ella grinned and nodded. Maddy was already looking through some of the things I had set out on the counter: notebooks and pencils, plus cookbooks and computer printouts of possible French recipes we could make.

"So, where do you think we should start?" I asked my friends.

Before they could answer, Mom stepped into the kitchen, a spiral binder under her arm and a pen in hand. "So you girls are going to start baking this morning? And do you have a business name yet?"

I met my friends' eyes, and we all said in unison, *"La Petite Pâtisserie."*

Mom smiled. "I like it! Well, I'm here if you need me. And let me know when you're ready to use the oven, okay?" Then she turned back to the living room with her folder full of lesson plans.

"Thanks, Mom," I said as I dug through the recipes on the counter. I pulled out one for a French yogurt cake that I wanted to show my friends. Ella and Maddy drew close, reading it.

"Yogurt cake?" Ella said, scrunching up her face.

I nodded. *"Gâteau au yahourt. Gâteau* means 'cake' in French."

"O . . . kay," Maddy said, in a way that made me uncomfortable.

"In France," I went on, "this is a recipe kids learn to bake when they're as young as three years old. They use a yogurt container, not only for its yogurt, but then to measure the other ingredients with the container. It makes it super easy for little kids to get started in the kitchen."

"I'm pretty sure we know how to *measure*, Grace," Maddy said.

"I know." I paused. "It's just that, well, I thought it might be a fun way to get started. It's French. Plus it's delicious. And we already have everything we need, so we could get started right away."

I looked at Maddy, and then at Ella.

"Why not?" Ella said.

"Yeah, okay. I'm in," Maddy agreed, removing the hair band from her wrist and gathering her red mane into a ponytail. "Let's get started."

A little over an hour later, Mom took our little golden cake out of the oven. We invited her out to the deck to be our first customer.

Once Mom was seated at the round table, I brought out a tablecloth we had bought together at a Paris street market—with blue flowers printed on vivid yellow—and flapped it in the air, then let it settle on the table in front of her.

"Voilà, Madame!" I said, using my best French accent.

Then I plucked a single red tiger lily from the nearby garden, and hustled back into the kitchen for a vase before setting the flower on the table in front of Mom.

"Lovely," she said. "It's like I'm back in Paris."

"That's the idea," I said.

Then I helped Ella and Maddy carry out four slices
of warm cake, four glasses of cold milk, plus four
forks and napkins—and we sat down. I eyed the des-
sert. Something was missing to make it extra special.
"Wait!"

I jumped back up, raided the refrigerator, and came
back with a bowl of raspberries.

"Garnish!" I said, sprinkling red raspberries over
each slice of cake. The red against the honey-colored
cake was just what it needed.

"I can't wait to try it!" Maddy said, fork in hand.

"Customers first," I said, trying to sound sweet, not
bossy.

Maddy paused. "Right," she said, although I could
tell it was killing her to wait.

"Now may I try it?" Mom asked, with a smile.

We all nodded.

She lifted the fork to her lips and tried a bite of
gâteau au yahourt with fresh raspberries, closing her
eyes. She didn't say a word, but went straight for a
second bite, again closing her eyes.

"Well?" I asked, leaning in.

"Do you like it, Mrs. Thomas?" Ella chimed in.

"Do you love it?" Maddy added.

Mom beamed. "It's wonderful!"

Then we all dove in for a taste, too. The cake was warm, moist, and delicious—*La Petite Pâtisserie*'s first success!

"Oh, yum!" Maddy exclaimed.

"It's really good," Ella added.

I smiled and high-fived with my friends.

A surge of energy filled me from head to toe. This was just the beginning, but at last, we had launched!

I couldn't wait to tell Grandma and Grandpa about *La Petite Pâtisserie*. They were the ones who had inspired me to start a business, after all. So that afternoon, I walked Bonbon over to First Street Family Bakery. I tied her leash to a post just outside the front door, where I could see her through the window.

Grandma spotted me and opened the front door. "Grace, sweetie. Come in. What a perfect time for a visit—there aren't any customers at the moment.

Actually, it's been unusually quiet today. So it's extra nice of you to come by!"

Before I'd taken more than a few steps into the bakery, I'd already told Grandma about the French cake my friends and I had made. "A *gâteau*," I said, pronouncing it carefully.

"That's wonderful, Grace," Grandma said, kissing the top of my head. "You certainly are filled with ideas—and ambition! If you're going to run a business, you'll need both. And if you need help with anything else along the way, just ask Grandpa and me, okay?"

I nodded. "Actually, I did come to ask for something."

"Oh?" Grandma paused. "Sure, Grace. What do you need?"

"You know all those aprons you've collected that you keep in the back room? I was just wondering if I could borrow some for my friends."

Grandma smiled. "Of course! They just sit in a bag most of the time. And you've probably worn every single one of them at some time or another, don't you think?"

I nodded proudly. From the earliest that I could

remember, I had loved to visit the bakery. At first I could only watch my grandparents bake, but even then I'd insisted on wearing an apron.

"I'll keep an eye on Bonbon while you head into the kitchen," Grandma said. "You know where the aprons are. Your grandpa's cleaning up for the day. And he'll be happy to see you."

I gave Grandma a quick hug and then hurried past the counter into the kitchen.

Friday morning, my friends and I met again at ten o'clock.

Same time, same place.

Bonbon reluctantly went into her crate and lay down.

"Just for a while," I reassured her, turning back toward Maddy and Ella.

My friends and I sorted through one French recipe after another, trying to agree on what to bake next. Finally, after a half hour had passed, we settled on *madeleines.*

"They're like little cookies named after me," Maddy joked. Her full name is Madeline.

"Perfect!" I said. "And better yet, I can finally use the *madeleine* baking pans Mom helped me find in Paris." They were like cupcake pans, but instead of round cups, or "wells," these wells were oval, shallow, and scalloped like a seashell.

I pulled out the canvas bag filled with Grandma's aprons. They were worn soft with age, but all the familiar colors and patterns were like treasures to me. "Go ahead and pick one," I said, holding the bag out to my friends.

Ella chose a pink floral apron, and Maddy found one with a bluebird with musical notes coming from its open beak.

Then we washed our hands and set to work gathering ingredients, following directions, and mixing the batter up in a bowl. Mom helped us melt the butter, and I carefully grated the rind of a fresh lemon for the zest, which also went into the batter.

But when it came time to fill the pans with batter, my friends and I each had different ideas about how to do it.

The directions said to fill each well in the pan "almost halfway full with batter."

I filled the first well with a little batter.

"That isn't enough," Maddy said. She added another large spoonful, which made the batter brim at the edge. As she took the spoon away, she dripped batter across the pan.

"But that's *too* much," I said. "The *madeleines* have to have room to expand." As I wiped away the excess drips of batter from the pan, I added, "Plus, Maddy, can you try to be a little more careful?"

"Picky, picky," she replied.

We stared at each other for a moment, until Ella said, "How about if we do an experiment with the first pan? There are twelve wells in the pan, which means we can each fill four of them our own way."

"Fine by me," said Maddy, and I agreed.

As we set to work filling the wells, I felt as if we were the three bears: Mama, Papa, and Baby Bear. I filled my four wells with what I thought was the right amount of batter. Maddy added a lot more, and Ella filled hers somewhere in between mine and Maddy's. We wouldn't know until the pan came out of the oven which baker had it just right.

When the oven reached the right temperature and started beeping, Mom came in from the deck, where she was—what else—working on lesson plans for her new class of fourth-graders. As she reached for the baking pan to put it into the oven, she paused, examining the pan. She scrunched up her lips, as if ready to say something.

"Mom, we know," I said. "They all look different. It's an experiment."

"Uh, okay," she said hesitantly as she closed the oven door.

While the *madeleines* baked, Maddy, Ella, and I held off on filling the next pan. We wanted to see how the first pan turned out! Instead, we filled a sink with soapy water and cleaned up the bowls and measuring spoons. When we finished that, we started looking over other recipes for everything from *tartelettes* to *éclairs*.

Suddenly the sweet smell of *madeleines* baking turned bitter. Smoke spilled from the oven, and the smoke alarm went off. *Beep! Beep! Beep!*

"Mom! Emergency!" I called out the window to the deck, knowing that I wasn't allowed to yank whatever was burning out of the oven on my own.

Beep! Beep! Beep!

As the smoke alarm shrieked overhead, Bonbon clawed frantically at her crate door. A crate is supposed to help calm dogs down, but clearly it wasn't working. I opened the door to let her out.

Bonbon raced out of the crate and around the counter so fast that her little legs slipped out from under her and she slid on her side. Frantic, she sprinted toward the screen door at the same moment that Mom came rushing in.

Beep! Beep! Beep!

As Mom stepped into the kitchen, Bonbon bolted outside.

"Oh no!" I cried. "Mom, I have to go after her." I looked around for my shoes, hoping I could get outside before Bonbon escaped through one of the gaps in the stone wall.

But Bonbon was the furthest thing from Mom's mind right now. She grabbed two hot-pads and flung open the oven door. She pulled out a pan with a small lava flow running over the side—charred and smoking.

Beep! Beep! Beep!

"I'm sorry, Mrs. Thomas!" Maddy called above the alarm. "The batter must have overflowed. I put in too much!"

I slid into my flip-flops as Mom threw open the kitchen window to let the smoke out.

Frantic, I stepped outside onto the deck and scanned the flower gardens, the yard, and the base of each tree.

My stomach twisted.

Bonbon was nowhere to be seen.

Dog in Training
Chapter 5

*B*onbon!" I called.

My heart sank. I remembered when she'd stopped showing up outside the *pâtisserie* in Paris. I'd been putting out bowls of food and water for her every night, and then one day she just didn't show up.

She didn't know Bentwick—or even this new house and neighborhood—very well yet. And that stupid fire alarm had scared the living daylights out of her. What if in her panic, she'd raced off and gotten lost? I couldn't bear to lose her twice.

"Bonbon!"

I raced through the gap between the stone wall and the house and around to the driveway. "Bonbon!" I called. But there was no sign of her.

Just then, a shrill yipping and yapping rose beyond our yard—the sort of sound Bonbon had

made when she'd first met Ella's dog, Murphy. I ran
back around the house, and just as I reached our backyard, I spotted her.

"There you are!" My heart settled back into my
chest.

Next door, in the middle of Mrs. Chatsworth's
backyard, Bonbon was nose to nose with Zulu, whose
golden body was three or four times as tall. But that
didn't seem to matter to Bonbon. She zipped around
Zulu, dashing one way and then the other, trying to get
her to play. Bonbon dropped her head to her paws with
her tail up in the air, wagging.

On her cable, Zulu made mock dashes at Bonbon.

I drew a breath of relief.

"Oh good," I said. "You're going to be friends.
But this playdate will have to wait." I reached down,
scooped up Bonbon under my arm, and carried her
back to our house.

Zulu whined and barked as we left.

"Found her," I said, returning to the kitchen. The
alarm had stopped beeping and most of the smoke had
cleared. Though Bonbon fought me, I put her back in
her crate, which would be the safest place for her until

things got back to normal.

Mom was helping Maddy turn the *madeleines* out onto a foil-covered countertop.

Some were underbaked—the ones that Maddy had overfilled. Some were overbaked—the ones that I had underfilled. And some looked just right—Ella's. She was nice enough not to say "I told you so."

With the next batch, we followed Ella's example, filling the wells half full. Then we watched them carefully through the oven window, looking for the moment when the edges had just started to brown and the top halves popped up.

After Mom pulled the second batch of *madeleines* out of the oven, we let them cool and then sprinkled them with powdered sugar. They looked perfect!

When we tasted the soft, lemony cookies, we all agreed that they were perfectly delicious, too.

"We should get some reviews," Maddy said.

"Reviews?" Ella asked.

"You know, people telling us what they think," Maddy said. "We should each take some *madeleines* home for our families to taste and have them write down what they think. If we get good reviews, we can print them in our brochures. It'll be really good advertising!"

Brochures? I hadn't thought about advertising yet, but if our business kept going well, we *would* need those someday. "I like it," I said. "Good thinking, Maddy."

Before Ella and Maddy headed home, I waved them over to the computer at the window. "Can we make a schedule for when we get together to work on our business?" I asked, opening my online calendar for August.

Maddy took off her apron. "Seriously? I hate schedules. Do we really need to put this on a calendar, Grace?"

I stared at my calendar for a minute, feeling my cheeks flush hot. What was with Maddy? It seemed as if just when things were going well between us, we would suddenly hit a brick wall. "What's wrong with some planning?" I asked, trying to keep my voice steady.

Maddy shrugged. "I just think it's more fun if we wing it," she said. "Don't you, Ella?"

Ella looked from me to Maddy, and then she slowly

untied her apron from around her waist. She pulled it off over her head and carefully returned it to the canvas bag.

"Ella?" I asked.

Finally she answered. "In a way, you're both right," she said, avoiding my eyes. "As soon as you put us on a schedule, it turns this into a chore. It becomes something we *have* to do. But if we don't put it on a schedule, we might not get anything done."

I thought of Mom, whose lesson folder had been practically glued to her side since we returned from Paris. "But teachers can't start a new year without planning ahead," I said. "Why is our business any different?"

"Because we're *kids*," Maddy said. "That's what's different. And this is supposed to be *fun*."

I sighed in frustration. "I guess I just do better when I have a plan, that's all." I looked at Maddy and Ella. "Can we just *try* to put things on a calendar? It won't be set in stone. We can change it anytime."

"Okay, fine," Maddy replied. "But Grace, we already know we're showing up again tomorrow morning. Ten a.m., right?"

Dog in Training

Ella shook her head. "I can't. I have to help with my brothers tomorrow morning, but I can meet later."

See? I wanted to say to Maddy. *This is why we need a plan.*

"When?" I asked Ella.

"Um, around two o'clock should work," she said.

"Is that okay with you, Maddy?" I asked carefully.

She nodded halfheartedly. I imagined that if she were a cat, she'd be flicking her tail in irritation.

I felt a sinking feeling in my stomach. I really wanted this business to work, but working with friends was turning out to be harder than I'd thought.

"I think I got spoiled in Paris," Mom said as she cooled down on the deck after her early Saturday-morning run.

"How so?" I asked, trying to keep a firm grip on Bonbon's leash even though I was still groggy and half asleep. Owning a dog meant a lot more work and responsibility than I'd realized. When Bonbon started whining and yipping to go outside every morning,

I had to get out of bed, whether I felt like getting up or not.

"In Paris," Mom said, leaning against the deck railing to stretch her legs, "you biked with me nearly every time I ran. Now, without you, each mile just feels a little harder. I miss your company." She smiled.

"I know," I said, sounding a teensy bit whiny. "But I can't walk Bonbon *and* bike with you every morning."

"I know, honey," she said.

As Bonbon pulled me along toward Dad, who was weeding the flower garden at the edge of the yard, I called back, "Mom, I'd love to bike and have her just run alongside me, but she's hard enough to *walk* on a leash."

I tried the treat method again, and the moment my hand went to my pocket, Bonbon ran back to me and dropped her rump to the ground, her eyes on me.

"Looks like she's making progress," Mom called.

"Yes, but I'm afraid the second she spots a squirrel or another dog, she'll be pulling me along like a train engine."

Mom laughed. "She'll learn, eventually. Till then,

Grace, don't worry about joining me in the morning. Staying motivated is *my* job. Not yours."

I tried to stay close to the deck so that I could keep talking with Mom, but Bonbon twisted and pulled at the end of the leash, as if trying to get away. "Mom, she needs to burn off some energy. Is it okay if I walk her on the towpath?"

"Sure," she said. "There are a lot of walkers and joggers out this morning. Just turn around before you reach town."

"Okay," I said, leading Bonbon through the gap between the stone wall and the house.

As we set off on the path, a zillion birds sang from leafy trees. I recognized the oriole and the bluejay. When a robin hopped along on the ground ahead of us, Bonbon strained at her leash toward it.

"No, you can't play with the robin," I said, calling her back to me with a treat.

I discovered again how strong she could be—and that treats don't last forever. When I reached into my pocket, the dog treats were all gone.

Now, with each passing walker, biker, or leashed dog, Bonbon tried to pull out of my hands. Walking her was exhausting. I already had one blister on my hand. How many treats was it going to take for Bonbon to learn?

As we rounded a bend in the path, I sucked in my breath. There was a great blue heron on stilt-legs, dipping its long beak into the river.

I tried to turn around, but Bonbon had already spotted the big bird. She started yapping.

"Bonbon, no barking," I said firmly.

But it didn't help. The heron flapped into the air and flew away.

"Aw, Bonbon, you ruined it!" I scolded. But she was already on the trail of something else, and all I could do was follow.

We passed several houses, their backyards butted up on either side of the canal. Some had steps or small bridges leading to their yards. At one, under an arch heavy with English ivy, I spotted a bike trailer, the kind parents use to bike with small children. This one was bright yellow nylon with blue trim over a metal frame that tilted sideways. One of its two wheels was gone. Taped to the trailer's side was a piece of cardboard that read: FREE.

◁ Dog in Training ▷

Wait. Maybe I couldn't expect Bonbon to trot nicely on a leash alongside my bike, but she was certainly small enough to fit inside a bike trailer. "You could bike with me! If we can get it fixed . . ."

I spun around and headed back home at a jog, with Bonbon trotting at my side.

"Josh!" I said, rushing into the kitchen. He was spooning cereal with sliced bananas into his mouth.

He glanced up at me, his mouth full.

I was out of breath. "I . . . I found the perfect thing for Bonbon so she can bike with me. A bike trailer that kids ride in. It's free, but I need you to look at it. It's missing a wheel and looks a little beat up, but if you could fix it, then . . ."

Mom stepped into the kitchen with wet hair, smelling of ginger-orange shampoo. "Then you could bike with me!" she said, finishing my sentence. "Oh, that's a great idea."

Josh looked from Mom to me. "I'm heading to the bike shop right now," he said. "I don't really have time."

"It's on your way. Just look, okay?" I pleaded. "I'll trade doing dishes if you can fix it."

Josh shrugged. "Okay. I'll look. But no promises."

"Thanks!" I said. As I unhooked Bonbon's leash, I was already imagining our first bike ride together—my little friend in the trailer behind me instead of trying to race up ahead. She'd still need walks, but now I could bike with her, too. It would be perfect!

The Sleepover
Chapter 6

*A*t two o'clock, Ella and I were ready to get going on our next baking project. But Maddy was nowhere in sight.

Ella and I waited five minutes, and then ten. While we waited, I told her about the bike trailer I had spotted on the towpath.

"Cool!" she said. "Is Josh going to be able to fix it?"

I shrugged. "I don't know."

"Send him a text," she suggested.

So I did. But the reply that came five minutes later wasn't what I'd wanted to hear: "Sorry, Grace," he wrote. "The trailer wasn't there anymore. Someone must have taken it."

So much for my great plan, I thought. But then I reminded myself of what I'd learned in Paris: We can't plan for everything. Sometimes we just have to "stay loose" and take things as they come.

I told myself that again when Maddy finally strolled in—half an hour late.

"Sorry," she said, but she didn't really *sound* sorry.

Then, as if she didn't see the bowls, spoons, and recipes spread out on the counter, she said, "Hey, let's start by designing the brochures we talked about! I have lots of ideas for those."

I cut her off right away. "How can we design brochures," I asked, "when we don't even know what we're making yet?"

I couldn't help feeling irritated. We'd already wasted so much time today!

Ella added softly, "I think Grace is right. We should start by trying a few more recipes first."

Maddy's face flushed a little. "Fine," she said, putting up her hands. "I guess I'm outnumbered."

Ella and I exchanged a glance.

"Okay, so . . . I was thinking we should write down the ingredients we'll need for a few more recipes, just in case we need to go shopping," I said. "Maddy, do you want to write the list?"

I offered her a notebook and pen—and was relieved

when she actually took them.

As Ella and I looked through recipes, Maddy jotted down the ingredients we would need. She spent more time, though, doodling distractedly in the margins of the notebook.

"It looks like we need to go to the store," I said, looking at our growing list.

Ella winced a little, and I suddenly remembered her situation. She didn't have any money to put toward supplies.

"Ella, will you be our record keeper for now?" I asked her. "You can keep track of what we spend on supplies, and when we start making money, you can pay us back—just like we talked about."

"Record keeper?" she said. "Yes! I like the sound of that. And I have the perfect notebook to use for it at home."

Maddy perked up, too. "I can run home and pull some money out of my piggy bank," she said. "Let's go shopping!"

Before I knew it, Ella and Maddy had dashed home on their bikes.

When my friends returned, Maddy and I pooled

our money together on the counter. As we counted the money, Ella showed us the notebook she had brought from home. It *was* perfect, with a cute cupcake on the cover. Above the cupcake she wrote the words *"La Petite Pâtisserie."*

"It looks almost official," I said, beaming. It felt good to be moving forward again with my friends—finally.

At the City-Way supermarket, Dad grabbed us a shopping cart—and then pulled out a second one for himself and Mom.

"We need a few things, too," Dad said. "You girls start looking and come find us if you need help, okay?"

"Will do," I said.

Just inside the doors, past the stand of flower bouquets, the store's newly remodeled bakery was busy with customers. They were lined up three deep at the counter.

"Psst!" I said to Ella and Maddy. "Let's go spy and

see what the new bakery's doing right."

We wove in and out of the crowd, peeking at all the desserts behind the glass. We saw cupcakes, cookies, and birthday cakes. There were doughnuts, doughnut holes, muffins, and breads—but nothing that looked out of the ordinary. So why was it so much busier here than at First Street Family Bakery?

I waved Maddy and Ella back toward the greeting card section.

"It seems like they make pretty much the same stuff as most bakeries," Ella said.

"Nothing really unique," Maddy agreed.

"Nothing *très* French," I said with a smile.

Then Ella pointed to a big sign we'd missed hanging from the ceiling:

Everyday City-Way deal:
Buy one, get one free.
Buy a dozen, get a dozen free!

Ella studied the sign. "Wow. That's a good deal."

"Bargain prices," I said. "But nothing like French pastries and treats. That's why we need to make things people can't get here or at another bakery."

We went back to our shopping, satisfied that we were on the right track with *La Petite Pâtisserie*. With Mom and Dad's help, we found most of the items on our list, but not everything.

Dad studied our list as we waited in line at the checkout. "Girls, it looks like you'll need a few more things to get your French baking business off the ground."

"Shhh!" I said, glancing at the line behind us.

"What?" Dad asked, wrinkling his brow.

"Mr. Thomas," Maddy whispered, "we don't want other kids to steal our business idea."

"Oh," Dad said. "I see."

Mom suggested we make one more stop: the Kitchen Shop.

She introduced us to the shop's owner, a man with a bright green vest and a ready smile. "Mr. Hammond," Mom said, "these girls want to start doing some French baking. Can you help them find what they need?" She handed him our shopping list.

"But of course," he said, leading us to his French section.

⚬ The Sleepover ⚬

In no time, Mr. Hammond helped us find parchment paper, a couple of special pans, and a pastry bag with tips. "This will get you started," he said. "You can always come back for more."

"*Merci beaucoup!*" I said as we left.

"You're welcome!" he replied.

When we returned home, Bonbon acted nearly as excited as we were to unpack our supplies. She raced in circles around us before I caught her and leashed her to take her outside.

Mom started putting things away in the refrigerator as Ella and Maddy reached for their aprons.

"Sorry, girls," Mom said, glancing over her shoulder. "It's getting too late in the day to let you take over the kitchen right now."

I looked at Ella and Maddy. "But, Mom, we had plans."

"And so do I," she said. "Like making dinner."

Just when we were ready to launch into baking, our plans screeched to a halt. I could almost imagine Mom holding up a big red stop sign.

I knew we couldn't take over Mom's kitchen, but there *had* to be a way to share it. I glanced at the clock and thought hard, and a solution came right away. Maybe today we could bake *after* supper instead of *before*.

"What if we do a sleepover?" I flashed Mom a smile. "Then after dinner, we could get started. Could we, Mom?"

"Wow, when you get an idea, you don't easily let go, do you, Grace?" she said, pulling lettuce, grated cheese, and tortillas out of the refrigerator.

"I think I get it from you, Mom." What could she say to that? It seemed true as far as I could see.

"Okay, sure," she said. "If you girls like tacos and your parents say yes. And if you can get Bonbon outside before the poor little thing has an accident."

I glanced down at the little dog, who was circling my feet. "Oh, sorry, Bonbon!" I opened the door and raced outside after her.

Mom agreed to our putting up a tent outside to sleep in. First, we found the nylon bag on a garage shelf, and then we carried it beneath the shade of the oak tree and slid out the tent and poles.

For a moment, we all just stared at the pile, unsure of what to do. It reminded me of the first time we were together in the kitchen.

To make things go better between us, I suggested we try something new. "What if we divide up jobs?" I asked. "One of us could put the poles together while the other two spread out the tent."

Maddy reached right in to grab a couple of metal poles and started clicking them together. Ella and I spread the tent across the ground and then found the nylon sleeves that the poles slid into.

We all had to work together to get the poles through the sleeves, but pretty soon the whole thing popped up like a giant orange mushroom. Then we took turns doing the fun part: hammering stakes into the ground at the tent's edges.

"Wow, we worked really well together," I said, admiring our results. If we could only learn to work that well as a team in the kitchen, our business could be amazing!

As we stepped inside the tent to roll out our sleeping bags, the sun glowed through the tent walls, and for a few moments, everything seemed possible.

After a dinner of tacos and fruit salad, we cleaned up the kitchen, only with plans to mess it up again.

Then we leaned over the recipes we wanted to try, spread out on the counter like road maps. I wanted to start with fresh peach *tartelettes*, but Maddy leaned toward *macarons*, and Ella wanted to try *crêpes* with different fillings.

I didn't care so much which recipe we tried. I was already thinking about what came next.

"Maybe we should split up jobs again, like we did with the tent," I said. "To me, there are three big jobs: Getting things ready—or prep work. Mixing and rolling out dough—or actual baking work. And cleanup. I'm thinking, let's each pick one area we are in charge of, and then the next time we bake, we can rotate—we can take turns at each job."

"That works for me," Ella said with a nod.

"And we can't spend all our time deciding what to bake each time," I added, checking the clock. "So maybe the person who does prep should just pick the recipe."

I glanced up at Maddy, who seemed too quiet all of a sudden. She stood straight and bristly as a broomstick. Her lips were clamped tight. *What's she unhappy about now?* I wondered. *Doesn't she get it?*

Ella must have noticed, too, because she said brightly, "Maddy, do you want to take prep this time? Then we can try *macarons,* like you wanted."

Maddy exhaled slowly. "Sounds fine," she said, but not very enthusiastically. "Let's get started."

She began reading off the ingredients we'd need from the recipe. "Sugar."

I opened the door of the cupboard where we kept our dry baking goods, and Ella reached for the bag of sugar. "Check," she said after placing the sugar on the counter.

Bonbon trotted in from the living room and pawed at my leg, wanting to play. "Not now," I said.

"Eggs," said Maddy.

I opened the refrigerator door. "Check."

"Flour," Maddy said.

But just as Ella turned from the cupboard with

half a bag of flour, Zulu barked from the yard next door, and Bonbon dashed across the kitchen right in front of Ella.

Ella tottered and lost her balance. As she went down, the bag of flour slipped from her hands.

"Ella!" I cried.

The bag hit the floor with a *thud* and erupted like a volcano. White flour spewed into the air, settling across the floor and the kitchen cabinets.

As I rushed toward Ella, I tripped over Bonbon's water bowl, sending a stream of water across the kitchen floor. Bonbon—terrified by the clatter of the bowl—slipped and slid right across that floury mess as she raced out of the kitchen.

"Bonbon!" I called. But before I could catch her, Dad's voice rang out from the living room.

"What in the world?! Grace! Get your dog!"

Josh dashed in from the garage. "What's going on?"

Bonbon heard the opened door and came tearing back through the kitchen, bolting right past Josh into the garage. I darted after her, but the garage door was wide open to the night. "Bonbon!"

This time, I knew where to look. I rounded the house and found Bonbon nose to nose with Zulu, who began to lick flour from Bonbon's fur. "Thanks, Zulu," I said, "but I'll give her a real bath."

I carried Bonbon back through the garage, where Josh's latest bike project was dismantled and spread across the floor like dinosaur bones.

"Good luck with that," I said, nodding at his project.

"Yeah, and good luck with *that*," he replied, as I stepped into the house with a very dirty dog.

In some ways, my whole idea of launching a business had become even more messy and overwhelming than Josh's bike project. There were so many pieces that had to come together to make it all work.

I wondered if my friends and I would ever get any further than buying a few things at the grocery store and baking a few recipes. Right now, turning baking into a real business seemed nearly hopeless.

I went directly to the laundry room and plopped Bonbon into the utility sink. "I'm in here if anyone needs me!" I called out to the kitchen.

"You look like you've been dipped in white chocolate," I told Bonbon as I filled the sink with warm water.

I scrubbed her with tearless oatmeal dog shampoo until her black spots and black button nose returned to normal. When I wrapped her in a towel, she shook her way right out of it, but I managed to dry her off at least a little bit.

When we returned to the kitchen, I put Bonbon in her crate and closed her door. "You have to be *all* the way dry before you're going anywhere," I told her.

Then I turned to my friends, who were on their hands and knees beside a scrub bucket, working flour paste off the floor and the bottoms of the kitchen cabinets. Flour is an amazing baking ingredient, but it's a real headache to clean up.

Mom was scrubbing the floor, too, in one of the farthest corners of the kitchen. Had the flour made it all the way over there?

"Thanks for helping," I said to her.

She glanced over her shoulder at me and gave me "the look," so I immediately added, "You can stop now, Mom. We'll take care of it."

The Sleepover

She didn't hesitate to hand me her sponge.

My friends and I kept at it, rinsing out the flour-turned-clay bits from our rags and sponges. We rinsed and washed and rinsed again until the kitchen was sparkling clean.

"There!" I said as we put away the bucket and our supplies. "Good as new. Now we can go back to making *macarons*!"

I glanced at the clock. It was already 7:45. I shot Mom a silent question.

In return, she shook her head. "Grace, I don't know what to say. I know you girls had big plans, but it's getting late. Why not start in tomorrow?"

"But Mom, we didn't *plan* to have an accident!" I said, trying not to whine.

"I know, but accidents happen, and sometimes we have to come up with a new plan," she said. "How about this? For tonight, instead of tackling a new recipe, why don't you stick to something quick and easy—maybe something you already know."

Maddy, Ella, and I glanced at one another. Then we put our heads together and whispered a few ideas—a baker's huddle.

"What can we do?" asked Maddy. "The only two recipes we've made so far are yogurt cake and *madeleines.*"

"Can we do *madeleines* with a twist?" suggested Ella. "Is there a way to make them taste different—or maybe look different?"

Bonbon whined from her crate, as if offering her two cents. "Speaking of looking different," I said, "you should have seen Bonbon before her bath. She looked like a pup dipped in white chocolate."

I laughed with my friends, but then suddenly stopped. "Wait . . . that's it!" I said loudly. "What if we dip some of the *madeleines* we already made in chocolate?"

"I love it!" Ella said. "I guess good ideas can come from accidents."

"You mean *disasters,*" Maddy added with a grin.

"I love it, too, Grace," said Mom, who must have overheard our conversation. "You came up with something easy that shouldn't take much time. This tired mom appreciates that."

Mom's eyelids did look a bit droopy. She'd put in ten miles that morning, and it was catching up to her.

Dad must have noticed, too, because he put a hand on her shoulder.

"Hey, I can help you girls melt the chocolate," he said. "And if you need a food critic—I'm your guy. I come with lots of tasting and eating experience."

Mom smiled with relief. "Oh good! Then I'm going to get into my pajamas early."

With a flashlight at hand, we settled into our sleeping bags in the shadowy tent. A mosquito buzzed and hummed around our heads, until Ella finally slapped it.

"I can't believe it's so late already," I said. "We spent the whole evening in the kitchen!"

"Baking takes time," Ella said. "But the *madeleines* dipped in chocolate were worth it. They were so delicious!"

"And Josh and your dad gave us great reviews," said Maddy, yawning. "I'm keeping a folder full of them for our brochures—I mean, for whenever we finally get around to making them."

Was Maddy still upset about not doing the brochures yet? I couldn't think about that right now—I was too happy. I just stared up at the tent ceiling, smiling. "I'm proud of us," I finally said.

"Yeah?" said Maddy.

"Yeah. We didn't give up tonight, did we?" I asked my friends.

"We didn't," Ella agreed.

A perfect, peaceful moment followed. Maybe we were all thinking about how hard we'd been working on our business this week.

Then I heard Maddy's heavy breathing from beside me. She must have fallen asleep.

I had started to nod off too when . . .

Scritch. Something brushed against the tent.

I sat up, my heart picking up speed. Was it a branch? But we'd pitched our tent clear of all the overhanging branches.

"What was that?" Ella said, rising to her elbow.

I listened. Crickets sang, high-pitched and comforting.

Scritch. Scritch. Again, the nylon fabric rustled.

Maddy woke up. "What *was* that?"

For a few moments, we heard nothing. Then the sound returned.

Scritch. Scritch.

Then came a weird sound, as if the wind were picking up just outside the door of our tent. But the tent wasn't moving. The night was still.

Whoooooooooo! Shooooooooo!

A tingle of fear tickled my neck.

And then came a low, spooky, and *familiar* whisper. "Falling, falling like a blizzard of snow . . . Flour is falling all around you . . . It's up to your knees and still it's falling, falling . . ."

"Josh!"

I snatched up the flashlight, clicked it on, and shined it out the screen door. The light lit up the grin on my brother's face.

"Josh! Quit trying to scare us."

"Hey, I just wanted to make sure you weren't having any nightmares," he said with fake sincerity. "You know, *baking* nightmares."

"Ha, ha, ha," I replied.

"The only nightmare is *you*," Maddy said, "trying to scare us half to death."

"*Brothers*," Ella added. "Grace, at least you have only one. Imagine having three!"

I snorted. "I *can't* imagine that." I lay back down in my sleeping bag, which suddenly felt cold and lumpy. "Thanks to you, Josh, now I probably won't sleep at all."

"Well, good night then, girls," Josh said overly nicely. "Sweet dreams."

When he was gone, my friends and I stayed awake for a while, replaying what we'd heard and what we'd each thought the sounds might have been.

"I was pretty sure it was a bear, sniffing out its next meal," Ella confessed.

Maddy took it a step further. "I heard a skeleton scratching the tent with its bony finger," she said in a spooky voice, which sent a shiver down my back.

"What did you think it was?" asked Ella, scooting a little closer to me.

"I had no idea," I said, "but I *should* have suspected Josh was up to another prank. He's so *not* funny."

But when I thought about Josh's words about flour falling like a blizzard, I started giggling—and that set Ella and Maddy off, too. Once we started giggling, we just couldn't stop.

The Sleepover

Finally I took a ragged breath to calm myself down, and wiped tears from my eyes. I couldn't remember the last time I'd laughed so hard with my friends. Everything felt like old times again between us.

I fought back a yawn. I didn't want this night to end!

A Hundred Flyers

Chapter 7

*A*fter the flour blizzard incident, Mom insisted that I crate Bonbon any time my friends and I were in the kitchen. But crating Bonbon was getting harder and harder!

On Sunday morning when I tried to put her in, she braced her front legs against the crate's doorframe and pushed back. I finally squeezed her in, shut the door, and said, "Sorry, Bonbon. Just for a little while—I promise."

She immediately began to paw at the metal door to get out.

"You're okay," I said. "I'm not keeping you in there forever."

But instead of settling in for her usual morning nap, Bonbon put her head on her paws, stared at me, and whined.

A Hundred Flyers

"Poor baby," said Ella as she tied on her apron.

We tried to ignore the whining as we wrapped up last night's batch of chocolate-dipped *madeleines*. Then I grabbed my tablet and motioned Ella and Maddy to the bay window near the kitchen table.

"Get comfy," I said.

With its red gingham pillows, the window seat was the perfect cozy place to read—or in this case, to watch cooking videos.

When we were all squeezed onto the seat together, I showed Ella and Maddy a list of online videos I'd discovered.

"Ooh, let's watch the *macaron* video first," Maddy said. "That was the next thing we were going to make, remember?"

The video was short, and it made *macarons* look pretty easy—*and* beautiful. The colorful little sandwich cookies looked just like the ones I'd seen in the windows of Paris *pâtisserie*s, each one perfectly matching the next.

Ella and I mixed up a batch of rose-tinted batter while Maddy spread out a sheet of parchment paper and began drawing little circles on it with a pencil.

"Wait, Maddy!" I said. "The video showed how to trace the circles around the cap of a bottle or jar, remember?"

Maddy paused, pencil in the air. "What's the difference?" she said. "I'm a good artist. I'm pretty sure I can draw circles that are about the same size."

But when I looked at the circles she had drawn, I could see that they weren't *exactly* the same size.

"Just do it the right way, Maddy, okay?" I persisted. "They won't turn out like the ones in the video otherwise."

"Wow, Grace, who made you the boss?" Maddy snapped. Her words hung in the air like the smell of burned batter.

Here we go again, I thought as we stared each other down.

"This might work," I said, quickly unscrewing the cap from an empty orange juice bottle on the counter. I washed and dried the cap, and then handed it to Maddy.

She took the cap, but she wouldn't look at me. I turned my back to her, too, to help Ella pour our batter into a pastry bag.

A Hundred Flyers

When it was time to turn over the parchment paper so that the pencil marks wouldn't touch the batter, I could clearly see Maddy's tracings. I tried to ignore the fact that a whole row of circles looked different from the other ones. We took turns *ooping* out the batter to fill the circles.

While we waited for the *macarons* to set, or to harden a little, I tried to lighten the mood. I started singing *"Frère Jacques"* while we mixed up the filling for the *macarons*.

Maddy stayed silent, but Ella joined in, which reminded me of singing rounds with Sylvie in Paris. The memory pinched at my chest. I missed my cousin! Bonbon began whining again. Was she missing Paris, too?

After a while, I touched the top of one of the *macarons*. I felt a hard skin, which meant that the *macarons* were ready to bake. "Perfect!" I announced. *"C'est parfait."*

Maddy groaned. "Grace, we *know* you went to Paris. Quit showing off."

Showing off? "I'm *not* trying to show off, Maddy," I said. "I just love the language, and if I don't ever use it, I'll forget what I've learned."

"But *'Frère Jacques,'* too?" Maddy said. "Aren't you going a little overboard?"

A thousand things to say went through my head, but none of them were very nice—or would help our business. So I stepped out of the kitchen and called for my mom to help put the *macarons* into the oven.

My friends and I waited in silence for a moment, until Ella—good old Ella—spoke up. "You're lucky to have a cousin who speaks French," she said to me. "I hope someday Sylvie can come here so that we can meet her, too."

I agreed. "That would be so cool."

Maddy, of course, said nothing.

Before noon, we'd somehow managed to create a batch of *macarons* mounded beautifully on a purple plate. They weren't all perfect—some of the circles were larger than others. But I'd tucked some of the mismatched ones on the bottom of the plate when Maddy wasn't looking.

⌒ A Hundred Flyers ⌒

I took out my phone and snapped a photo. *Click!*

Mom, Dad, and Josh sampled the first *macarons* while Ella, Maddy, and I hovered, waiting for their reactions.

Dad used his card-playing face as he sampled the first one. He kept his eyes down, his face stony and impossible to read. "Hmm . . ."

Josh did a drumroll with his fingers on the edge of the table.

"Well?" I asked, the anticipation killing me. "What do you think?"

My stomach clenched with waiting.

"Mmmm," Mom said after her first bite. "I see a growing problem . . ."

"What's that?" I asked, bouncing from foot to foot, hoping we hadn't made some drastic mistake in the recipe.

Mom pinched her waist and laughed. "But, wow, girls. These are delicious! Your *macarons* are a delight to the eyes and to the taste buds."

Josh grabbed a second *macaron*. "I'm not so sure," he said. "I need another shot at this." Then he practically swallowed the cookie whole.

"Mr. Thomas," Ella asked. "You haven't said anything yet. Don't you like them?"

"Hmm . . . I can't tell yet," he said. "Maybe one more." He grinned and grabbed another *macaron* from the plate.

Josh reached for a third. "For the road," he said, and then he headed for the door.

"Wait, Josh—we need your review!" I called out impatiently.

He paused in the doorway and raised his *macaron* like he was giving a toast. "I love 'em," he said before popping the cookie into his mouth.

I wrote down my mom's "Delicious! A delight to the eyes and to the taste buds!" and Josh's "I love 'em!" in our notebook so that we'd have them when we made brochures.

"Dad?" I said, as he finished his second *macaron*. "You have to tell us what you think."

"One word," he said. "*Divine.*"

With a smile, I glanced at Ella and Maddy. We'd done it! And then I added Dad's comment to our short but growing list of reviews.

Then I thought of something. I tore out the page of

reviews and handed it to Maddy. "Do you want to start designing the brochure, Maddy?"

It still seemed a little soon for a brochure. I mean, we had only made a few French treats so far. But I had to do *something* to try to fix things between Maddy and me.

Maddy cocked her head suspiciously. "But I thought you said it was too early for that, Grace," she said hesitantly.

I shrugged. "It doesn't hurt to get started, does it? And if you want, I can e-mail you photos of treats, too."

When Maddy nodded and reached for the page of reviews, Ella gave me a thumbs-up from behind Maddy's shoulder.

It was a small step toward making peace with Maddy, but it was something.

As scheduled, at exactly three p.m. (and nine p.m. in Paris), Mom and I stood at her computer, ready to video-chat with our French family. And sitting right in front of us were two special guests: Grandma and

Grandpa. This was their first time video-chatting, and I could feel their excitement.

When the connection was made, Sylvie and Aunt Sophie appeared, sitting side by side on their couch with Lily snug in my aunt's arms. I figured it was past her bedtime, but my aunt probably wanted to show her off anyway. Seeing them all in real time was the next best thing to being there.

"Oh, my! There's our lovely new grandbaby!" Grandma exclaimed.

"Hello, Mom!" Aunt Sophie called from the screen, waving at Grandma.

Grandpa just shook his head. "Well, isn't that something," he said. "You're right here!"

We all broke into smiles.

"Bonjour!" I said, waving at Sylvie.

"Hello, Grace!" Sylvie waved back. *"Bonjour, Grand-mère* and *Grand-père!"* she added shyly.

Baby Lily wanted to say hello, too. She began to coo like a little dove.

"Hi, Lily!" I said. "I miss you!"

At the sound of my voice, her arms and legs wiggled.

ᴄ A Hundred Flyers ᴐ

"She miss you," Sylvie said, practicing her English and offering her little sister a finger to hold on to.

"Look at that baby," Grandma exclaimed. "Oh, she's absolutely perfect!"

Aunt Sophie kissed the top of Lily's head and then looked up at the screen. "Thanks, Mom! We adore her."

"Sylvie," Grandma said, "you're a big sister now, aren't you?"

"*Oui, Grand-mère*," she replied with a shy smile. "How are you, *Grand-mère*?" I could tell she'd been practicing her English.

"I am just fine," Grandma replied. "And I'm so happy for your family!"

We all chatted using a little English, a little French, and lots of smiles. I was glad to see Sylvie getting to know her American grandparents—mine and hers— better at last.

Still, another part of me ached to have some alone time with Sylvie so that I could tell her how things were *really* going here—about the trouble I was having with Maddy, about how our new business was a lot harder than I'd thought it would be, and about Bonbon, who was having trouble adjusting to life here.

I wanted to step right through the screen into Sylvie's apartment and spend a few more days together, side by side. Video-chatting was good, but I couldn't breathe in Lily's soft baby scent or hang out with Sylvie and Colette in the warm *pâtisserie*.

Oh, why did we have to live so far apart?

On Monday afternoon, Ella and I parked our bikes outside Maddy's white Victorian house and climbed the steps to her wraparound porch, filled with wicker furniture. Everything about Maddy's house seemed elegant.

Maddy met us at the door, and then we stepped into a living room of white furniture, red satin pillows, and a towering bouquet of fresh flowers on the glass coffee table. The lamps, chandeliers, and fireplace trim were accented in gold.

Maddy's parents would love the Palace of Versailles, I thought, noticing the antique clock with two gold cherubs. But I kept it to myself. Maddy didn't need me bringing up all-things-French with every breath.

~ A Hundred Flyers ~

Besides, her parents had probably been to the famous palace, since they ran an expensive antiques store on Main Street, the kind where kids aren't really welcome. Whenever we'd stopped by with Maddy, she had asked us to wait outside while she checked in with her parents.

As we stepped through the living room, which was *très à la mode*, I realized that the house seemed eerily quiet.

"Anyone else home?" I asked.

Maddy shook her head. "My parents are both at the shop, but my mom will be back soon." Then she led us to the den, filled with bookcases and leather chairs. Above the chairs hung an ancient portrait of Maddy's relatives, all wearing black and staring sternly down upon us.

I could hardly blame them. This room was a mess! Paper was scattered here, there, and everywhere—on the desk, on the floor, and spilling from the printer. There were scraps and bits, the flurried remains of paper cutting and pasting.

But in the center of the computer desk, Maddy had placed a printed pamphlet. "This," she said, with a grand sweep of her arm, "is what I've been working on for the last few days."

Our business name, *La Petite Pâtisserie,* was printed on the cover of the pamphlet, with images of cakes, cupcakes, and doughnuts dancing around it. Inside was a list of all the baked goods we'd already made, with a photo of each and reviews from our family members.

"Maddy!" I exclaimed. "You're amazing!"

She shrugged, like what she'd done was no big deal, but I could tell from the creases at the edge of her green eyes that she was pleased. This was what she'd been dying to do, and she was really good at it!

Ella and I sat down to study the cover of the pamphlet. It was beautiful and looked really professional, but something kept niggling at me. We needed something really French and unique on the cover to go with our business name.

"Hey, I wonder if we could make this look more French somehow," I thought out loud. "I mean, we don't really make cupcakes and doughnuts. But could we find artwork of French pastries or make a French logo to go with our name?"

A Hundred Flyers

As soon as I saw Maddy's expression, I wanted to take back my words. Her face fell, and instead of looking mad, as usual, she just looked hurt. She had worked really hard on all of this, I could tell, and I had just burst her bubble.

Ella sprang to Maddy's defense. "*La Petite Pâtisserie* is French," she pointed out. "Maybe that's enough?"

A silence hung in the air, and I scrambled to fill it. "Yeah, this is great," I said with forced enthusiasm. "Let's go with what you have here, Maddy."

She nodded, but her smile looked forced, too. The damage was done.

It took us the rest of the afternoon to print a hundred flyers and carefully fold them all into thirds, with our business name on the front.

"Oh my gosh," Ella said, staring at the stacks. "This makes it feel real, doesn't it?"

"Sure does," I said.

"Should we hand them out tomorrow?" asked Maddy.

A mix of feelings fluttered through me. Passing out the flyers would set things in motion. What if this business took off like a kite in a strong wind? I worried it might get away from us.

But my friends looked so excited. I didn't want to be the one who brought everything to a stop. So when Maddy suggested meeting at her house in the afternoon and delivering the flyers on our bikes, I put on a smile and said, "I'm in."

In the Doghouse
Chapter 8

$\mathcal{T}$he next afternoon, backpacks loaded, Ella, Maddy, and I formed a bike brigade and started popping our pamphlets inside front doors around our neighborhood.

"Should we put them in mailboxes, too?" asked Ella.

"No!" Maddy called from up ahead. "I think that's against the law."

"Yikes!" said Ella, riding beside me. Then she grinned and said, "I can't believe we're actually doing this, Grace, can you?"

"I know," I said. "We're launching our business!" I was excited to be taking this big step. But something kept nagging at me. *Are we going too fast, getting ahead of ourselves?* I wondered.

Then I thought of when I'd first arrived in Paris. I'd been trying to plan ahead and learn the language, and

I was so worried about making mistakes. But I'd finally realized that sometimes jumping in feetfirst is the only way to learn. You can't plan for *everything*.

So I just kept going, tucking pamphlets behind doors and racing after my friends toward the next house. We worked our way up and down the streets of Bentwick, starting with the area around Maddy's home until we reached Ella's street and beyond.

We ran out of pamphlets, of course, long before we had reached every house, but it felt great to be under way!

After congratulating one another, we all split up to head home for lunch.

As soon as I got home, I took Bonbon out for a short walk. That's when my excitement began to fizzle and that nagging worry returned, growing and rising inside me like yeasty dough.

The pamphlets had our business name and a short list of French treats, along with descriptions and reviews. But at the last minute, right before printing the pamphlets, we'd realized that we needed a way for people to order from us. I'd suggested using my family's home phone number. I hadn't asked permission first, but I hoped that was okay.

My stomach twisted.

I *should* have asked for permission first.

I suddenly doubted it *was* okay.

I suddenly was *certain* my parents were not going to be happy, especially when they found out that we'd dropped a hundred pamphlets around town and the phone was about to start ringing.

I suddenly dreaded going home.

And the more I fretted about what we'd included, I realized we'd also left *out* some important information.

We'd forgotten to add prices!

As I reached the back deck of the house with Bon-bon, the phone rang inside. *Ring, ring, ring!*

I paused, my hand on the door handle.

"Hello?" Mom's voice floated out the open window. "Prices? I think you have the wrong number."

Pause.

"In your door? And that's where you found *this* number to call?"

Pause.

"No, I had no idea," Mom said. "Well, actually, my daughter and her friends have been baking and talking about starting a business, but I didn't really know it had gone this far."

Pause.

"Yes, you can say that again."

I mustered up some courage and stepped inside with Bonbon. The moment she dashed across the floor, I realized that I'd made another mistake. Bonbon left a string of muddy footprints in her wake.

"Don't worry, Mom," I said, glad for an excuse to turn away. "I'll get a rag and clean it up."

But as I turned toward the pantry, Mom held the phone at her side. "Grace."

"Yeah?"

"We need to have a serious talk after dinner. The phone's been ringing off the wall. You girls passed out pamphlets with *our* phone number on them?"

I swallowed hard and nodded.

Clearly, both Bonbon and I were in the doghouse.

While I waited for dinner, Bonbon joined me up on my bed—her dirty paws wiped clean. She could tell that something was wrong, and she stared at me with a "What are we going to do next?" expression.

"We're hiding out until dinner," I said. Chances were, Mom and Dad were going to tell me to stop my baking business. "It was one thing to have fun baking, but it is quite another," I imagined Mom saying, "to have strangers calling our house."

Bonbon tilted her head, as if trying to read my mind. I pressed my face into her neck and breathed in her sweet doggy smell.

"I just made a whopper of a mistake," I told her. "And I don't know how to fix it."

While Bonbon and I holed up behind my closed bedroom door, the phone rang four more times before dinner. With each phone call, a fizz of excitement swept through me. Were people calling to order our pastries?

But that excitement was quickly dampened by one glaring thought: *How could I have used our phone number without my parents' permission?* My friends and I had been in such a hurry to get the pamphlets printed and out to future customers. And in my rush, I'd lost my parents' trust.

I was a kid. Without my parents' support, I wouldn't

be able to run a real business. But I had no idea how to fix this mess. How can you make someone trust you again?

Bonbon licked my cheek.

"You didn't trust me at first, did you, girl?" I said, nuzzling her head. "But then I set out food and water, every night, and eventually you came around. Maybe that's it, huh, Bonbon? Maybe I just have to try to show my parents every single day that I can learn from my mistakes." What else could I do? I was out of ideas.

By the time Josh called me down to dinner, I felt as ready as I could be. I waited until we'd finished off our bowls of Caesar salad and Josh had nabbed the last piece of homemade pizza.

The moment he finished eating, he said, "I'm meeting up with Younkers and Spitz. We want to do some mountain biking on the north end of the towpath."

I flashed him an "I need you" look, but he missed it entirely. He just popped up from the table and took off.

Great. Leave me alone with Mom and Dad. I braced myself for "the talk."

Mom suddenly produced one of our pamphlets from out of nowhere and passed it to Dad. *Where did she get that from?* I wondered.

"Oh, I love the design," Dad said, examining the cover. "You girls have really taken this idea and run with it."

I didn't realize I had been holding my breath until that moment. I exhaled slowly, feeling the unexpected praise sink in. With a nod, I said, "We worked hard on those. But I apologize for not asking first."

He stared at me. "Apologize?" he said. "For what?"

Mom pointed to the phone number on the cover of the pamphlet. "Do you recognize that number?" she asked him. "The phone's been ringing off the hook. We have a lot of curious neighbors."

"That's good, yes? About the curious neighbors?" he asked, a weariness in his forehead. Sometimes when Dad returns from his job as a therapist, he seems a little out of it. "Listening with compassion," he once said, "takes a lot of energy." Now I could see what he meant.

"Our phone number," Mom repeated slowly, for Dad's sake. "We don't want to turn our home into a business office. At least *I* certainly do not."

"No," Dad said, as if suddenly coming around. "I don't either."

"I'm sorry I didn't ask," I said. "I didn't think it through. But we could use another number. Maddy's or Ella's?"

"Grace," Mom said, "I'm pretty sure their parents are going to feel the same way."

Dad leaned forward with his hands clasped, a sure sign that he was bringing his listening skills back into play. "Grace, have you thought about bringing in a few business advisers? In other words, *parents*? Or even your grandparents?"

I didn't like where this conversation was going. "But it's *our* business, Dad," I protested. "A *kids'* business. That's the idea."

"But as your business grows, it may benefit from some help," he continued. "It can't hurt, can it?"

I sighed. "Dad, but then it's not *ours*. I'm afraid you'll want to take over or something. Or tell us to quit."

Mom leaned forward. "At school," she said, "kids' clubs often have a teacher adviser. We have no interest in taking over or starting a business. But we might be able to point out a few things to consider as you go along."

In the Doghouse

I took a deep breath. *At least they aren't making me quit,* I reminded myself. And I had to show them that I had learned something from my mistake.

"Okay," I replied. "That sounds good. I . . . I was afraid you were going to make me quit."

Mom shook her head. "The Thomases aren't quitters," she said. "You've encouraged me not to quit training for my half marathon, haven't you?"

"That's right," added Dad. "We can't quit over a few bumps in the road, Grace."

I couldn't help it. I jumped up and gave Mom and Dad each a hug.

The Parents' Meeting
Chapter 9

*T*hursday night, our "advisers" gathered in our living room around a coffee table full of French pastries. Grandma and Grandpa were scrunched in around the table beside Mom and Dad. Ella's dad, Mr. Petronia, was sampling chocolate-dipped *madeleines*. Maddy's mom, Mrs. Eaton, was trying our newest item, fresh strawberry *tartelettes*.

Maddy, Ella, and I scurried around in our aprons and refilled coffee cups and lemonade glasses. We were trying really hard to "sweeten up" our parents after our big mistake, and so far, it seemed to be working.

Grandma wagged her head. "Just look at what you girls are accomplishing!"

Grandpa leaned forward, chuckling. "You're a chip off the old block, aren't you, Grace?" he said proudly.

"Ah, but you and I have never made French treats like these," Grandma said. "Grace, you girls must send photos to your Aunt Sophie and Uncle Bernard. They'll be amazed."

I beamed. "We already have!" I said, tapping my tablet. "And Sylvie's helped us, too. She's our French consultant. We e-mail back and forth."

"My goodness," Grandma said. "Technology is something, isn't it?"

"Speaking of technology," said Mom, "I'm sure none of us wants our personal phone numbers connected to the girls' business. But the girls need some way for customers to contact them and place orders. Any thoughts?"

Mrs. Eaton fiddled with the amber stone at the end of her silver necklace. "From our experience with our antiques business, the best way is to set up a website for advertising products and receiving order requests. As long as you don't take actual payments online, it's pretty easy to set up. We created our own website, and there's no reason why we can't help the girls launch their own, too."

Mrs. Eaton reached for her laptop beside the

couch and flipped it open. "We could even get started tonight—at least with a very basic design."

A website? Tonight? A hum of energy buzzed through me. I'd been worried about parents taking over our business, but now I realized how much they could *help* us.

"*La Petite Pâtisserie,*" Grandpa said, holding up one of the pamphlets. "I like it. You already have a name."

"The pamphlet's just a beginning," Maddy said hurriedly. "We, um . . . want to work on it some more." She cast a glance at me and then looked downward, which made me feel bad.

Things hadn't felt right between Maddy and me since I'd criticized her pamphlet cover. I still felt like it needed something more French, but I sure wasn't going to bring it up again.

"Great, Maddy," Mrs. Eaton said. "We'll transfer some of the information from your pamphlet onto the website tonight when we get home."

As Mom read the pamphlet information, she called out a few misspellings, which I had pretty much expected. "Misspellings make you look less professional," she said. "You should find someone to proofread everything you put in print."

"Want to volunteer, Mom?" I asked.

She laughed. "I guess I set myself up for that one. Sure."

Ella's dad—Mr. Petronia—was super helpful, too. In his Boston Red Sox T-shirt, he sat on the edge of his chair. "You know, girls, someone's always selling stuff to eat when my softball league plays a game. Maybe selling at games is a place to start . . ."

"Hmm . . ." said Mom. "That's a great idea—and it gives me another one. My half marathon is only a little more than two weeks away, but maybe you girls could set up a stand there, too?"

"Bentwick's Last Blast of Summer run?" I asked. I could barely contain myself. That would be an amazing place to launch our business.

I shot Mom a knowing smile. She'd be running her first half marathon, and we'd be selling at our first official event.

Ella and Maddy said in chorus, "Yes!"

Then Grandpa held up one of our pamphlets. "What about the matter of prices?" he asked gently.

"I know," Maddy groaned. "We completely forgot!"

"But how do we know what to charge?" I asked.

"A good rule of thumb," Grandma said, "is to add up your costs—your ingredients for a recipe—and then divide it by the servings the recipe makes. Then double that number to make sure you earn a profit on each treat sold."

"Wow, Grandma," I said. "You just proved that you don't have to be high-tech to be smart."

She winked at me.

"I think I can help lower the cost of your supplies," Mr. Petronia said. "I'm going to start raising a few chickens in our backyard. It's something fun to do while I look for a new job, and it means you girls can have eggs at a family discount. Or maybe for free when the chickens lay more than I get orders for. How does that sound?"

"That's great!" I added. "We go through a lot of eggs."

"So, let's see," said Grandma, tapping her chin as if running down a list of to do's. "What else? Well, let's not forget about packaging. You'll need a way to display your treats at the marathon. So we should add that to your supply costs. And Grandpa and I can show you how to make labels that list all your ingredients—customers want to know what they're eating, plus how to contact you . . ."

As the group started discussing costs, prices, packaging, and labels, my head began to whirl. Maddy looked just as dazed as I felt, but Ella had her head down in concentration. She was working on something in her notebook, where she kept receipts and a log of what we'd spent at the grocery store.

I was amazed when her head popped back up and she said she'd figured out some prices for our baked goods. "I followed your formula," she said to Grandma.

"Nice, Ella!" said Maddy. "Thank goodness one of us has some wicked math skills."

Ella smiled, her cheeks pink.

Then Mrs. Eaton said, "Speaking of prices and profits, we may want to start a bank account for what you earn through your business. And we'll want to look into licenses and taxes."

"Before we can get started?" I asked, feeling completely overwhelmed now. There was *so* much to think about. Couldn't we just get back to what we loved most: baking in the kitchen?

"I don't think you'll need to worry about those things right away," said Mrs. Eaton, "but I'll start looking ahead, in case your business takes off. That way there won't be any unpleasant surprises."

"It's good to look ahead," Mom agreed.

"What you *will* need soon," Dad chimed in, "is a suitable cart or table to sell from. Have you girls given that any thought?"

"A table sounds easy," Ella said, squeezing in beside her mom. "But a cart could be a little harder to find."

I must have looked worried, because Dad spoke up again. "Don't worry, Grace. We'll come up with something."

I gave him my most grateful smile. My friends and I could do a lot of this ourselves, but now we knew that it didn't hurt to have a *little* help.

When everyone left that evening, I felt totally exhausted. I flopped on the couch with Bonbon nestled beside me. She gave my chin a quick lick, as if to reassure me.

The Parents' Meeting

We still had tons of work to do! We needed to reprint pamphlets with our prices and website. We needed to buy small bags and boxes to package our treats. We needed to print labels for our packages with ingredients and contact information.

And what about the cart we needed for the half marathon—in just two weeks? I closed my eyes, almost wanting to cry.

Just then, the door from the garage to the kitchen squeaked open. "Is the coast clear?" I heard Josh ask.

"Everyone left," said Dad, "if that's what you mean."

"Good! I have a surprise for Grace."

At those words, Bonbon and I jumped up from the couch and raced into the kitchen. I suddenly felt a whole lot more energetic.

"I was going to wait until your birthday," Josh said when he saw me.

My birthday wasn't until September 17.

Josh continued, "But I didn't think *Bonbon* should have to wait that long."

Bonbon?

My little dog and I followed Josh back out into the garage, with Mom and Dad trailing behind us. And there, attached to the back of my bike, was a completely restored bike passenger-trailer with not one wheel, but two!

Instead of looking crooked and dirty, as the trailer had been when I had first spotted it along the towpath, now it was all cleaned up and polished and looked brand-new!

"*You* picked it up!" I burst out in surprise. "No wonder it was gone!"

"I figured I could fix it," Josh said, his face reddening. "My secret surprise."

Before I could say anything, Mom said it for me. "Hey, Grace! Now you and Bonbon can join me on my runs!"

I nodded happily and unzipped the mesh door to the bike trailer. I patted the inside. "Bonbon! Jump in!"

She looked at me through her pirate patch of fur, her head tilted as if I were asking her to walk the plank or something.

"You and I can bike with Mom," I said, enticing her, "and we can bike with Ella and Maddy . . ."

But my little dog just stared.

Finally, I picked her up and popped her inside. She

seemed fine for a moment, until I zipped the door back up. Though I could see her and she could see me, she started whining and scratching at the netting.

"No!" I said firmly, before she could tear it.

She crouched deeper into the trailer, looking scolded.

"It's okay, Bonbon," I said gently. "This is all new, I know."

I unzipped the opening, and she didn't waste any time jumping back out onto the garage floor. My stomach churned. I had a sinking feeling that this bike trailer wasn't going to work for me and Bonbon, but I couldn't let Josh see that.

"I'll work with her a little more so she gets used to it before we go for a ride," I promised him.

Josh looked so proud and happy. I think my brother loves fixing bike stuff as much as I enjoy baking in the kitchen. And he is good at it, too.

I looked more closely at the work Josh had done on the bike trailer, and that gave me an idea. "Josh, if we needed a baking cart that we could push, could you build it?"

He looked at me sideways. "I don't follow you."

"What she's saying," Dad said, "is that the girls need something for the half marathon. Something they could fill with their baked goods and sell from."

Josh hesitated. "I fix bikes," he said. "I don't really build stuff."

"But I'm pretty handy with a power saw," Dad said, a flash of excitement in his eyes. "Between the two of us, do you think we could try to help Grace out?"

Josh's eyebrows rose, and a slow smile inched across his face. "It's going to need wheels."

"Aren't you two forgetting something?" Mom said. "A wooden cart and wheels are a good start, but there's more to it than that. It's also going to need metalwork— and someone who knows how to weld."

"Who did you have in mind?" Dad asked playfully.

"Mom!" I said, thinking of all the sculptures she had welded out of metal—before she got so busy training for the half marathon. "But, Mom," I said again, "I know that you have tons going on and that you're super busy right now."

The edges of Mom's mouth turned up slightly. I think she appreciated that I understood.

"It's all right, Grace," she said, smiling. "A woman's

work is never done. Besides, I'd be happy to help."

"Great!" Dad said. "Looks like we have a construction team. This is going to be fun! But before we get going, we'll need ideas from you, Grace."

A yawn escaped me. "I'll get right on it," I said.

"Tomorrow," Mom said, coming to my rescue. "It's getting late."

The Delivery

Chapter 10

I wanted to try to run with Mom on Saturday morning, to help her during her last two weeks of training just like she was helping me with the baking cart.

But when I tried to get Bonbon back in the bike trailer, it was a *disaster*. First she braced her hind legs, and I had to push her in.

"Stay," I said.

She sat facing me as I zipped up the screen door.

Everything seemed okay until I hopped on my bike. "Ready, Mom," I said.

Mom set off jogging, and I started to pedal. But before I'd passed a half-dozen houses on the towpath, I could feel the trailer behind me starting to rock back and forth. Just as I stopped the bike, Bonbon ripped through the screen door, hopped out of the trailer, and

The Delivery

bolted down the path toward home.

"Mom, Bonbon escaped!" I cried. I waved her on ahead while I biked home to find Bonbon.

I was pretty sure I knew where I would find her. At least I *hoped* she would be there.

And she was.

Bonbon was playing in Zulu's yard. They both had their rumps up in the air, tails wagging, and their heads down on their paws, daring each other to make the first move.

"Bonbon, what am I going to do with you?" I groaned as I knelt down to scoop her into my arms.

I thought about putting her in her crate, but she'd been so hard to crate lately that I grabbed her leash instead. Then I found a needle and thread and brought Bonbon with me into the garage. She lay down, her guilty eyes on me as I tried to mend the bike trailer screen.

My stitches didn't look great, but I somehow managed to fix the screen. When I was done, I gave Bonbon a talk. "How can I ever take you anywhere fun," I asked her, "if you're going to claw your way free?"

She whined pitifully. Neither of us had answers.

Later that day, Ella and I met at Maddy's house to print out the brand-new pamphlets—the ones with our Web address and prices. On it we included the words: *For the most up-to-date menu, check out our website.* Our website was now up and running, thanks to Mrs. Eaton, and we wanted to get the word out about it.

Though it wasn't very exciting to retrace our steps, we dropped the pamphlets off again at all the same houses. Maddy suggested we drop a stack off at the Kitchen Shop, too, where we'd found our special pans and pastry-making supplies.

The owner, Mr. Hammond, examined a pamphlet in one hand and thumbed the hem of his yellow vest with the other, beaming. "So this is what you girls have been up to! Fantastic!"

"Would you mind having them on hand at your shop?" I asked.

"Not a bit," he replied. "I'll put them here on the counter."

The Delivery

Before we left, we couldn't resist wandering around the shop. There were so many fun supplies—some we recognized and others that were foreign to me. Then I saw a section with all kinds of packaging: boxes and bags of different sizes and colors, all designed to hold baked goods.

"Look at these!" I said, calling over Maddy and Ella. "These are just what we need."

But Maddy shook her head. "I think we should have our name—*La Petite Pâtisserie*—on all of our packaging. We'll have to order it online."

She seemed so sure, like there wasn't any other way to look at it. But I was pretty sure there was.

"That sounds expensive, Maddy," I said.

"But it's worth it!" she said. "That's what advertising is all about—getting your name out there."

Ella stayed silent, playing with a box lid. I knew she didn't have money to spend on personalized packaging, but she wouldn't say so.

"Look, Maddy," I tried again, "do we even have time to order packaging online? The half marathon is only two weeks away."

That's when I noticed Mr. Hammond hovering

behind us. He must have heard us bickering. "Questions, girls? Anything I can help you with?"

For a moment, everyone was staring at me. I hesitated. Then I shook my head. "No, thanks. We're fine."

When Mr. Hammond had gone back behind the counter, I whispered to Maddy, "I guess we'll just have to hold off until we can agree on what to do. Okay?"

Maddy responded with only one word: "Whatever."

As we biked home in silence, Ella was the one to try to make conversation. "I'm super excited," she said, riding between us, "because last night my dad brought home six hens—Rhode Island Reds. They're so pretty, but they seem a little nervous about being in a new place."

"Wow, what does Murphy think of them?" I asked.

"He gave them one look, but as soon as my dad scolded him, he backed away. And then one of the hens flew at him with its talons out, which scared him half to death."

"Oh, poor Murphy," I said.

"I know," Ella said. "He hid under the deck. So I'm more worried about him, actually, than I am about the chickens."

⌒ The Delivery ⌒

I nodded in understanding. After so many dis-
agreements with Maddy, I kind of felt like a scared dog
hiding under a deck to get away from the angry hen. I
was afraid that anything I did or said would set her off.

I snuck a peek at Maddy's face as she rode quietly
along. She looked so withdrawn. For a moment I wondered, *Does she feel the same way?*

Sunday morning, before Maddy, Ella, and I started
baking, Dad helped us go online to research ideas for
our bakery cart. We printed out a few images, and
Maddy even sketched out a design based on some of
what we saw. She drew big wheels and lots of heart-
shaped details. She wanted to keep going on it, and I
didn't want to hold her back—not after our disagree-
ment yesterday. But by the time we started baking, we
were already running late.

We had to be done baking by three and leave time
for cleanup and Mom's "absolute-and-no-exceptions
deadline" of four p.m. She wanted the use of her
kitchen back by then.

Period.

So we jumped in as quickly as we could, making *macarons* we could freeze ahead for the marathon. We needed to build up our supply of treats, or our "inventory," as Grandma and Grandpa called it.

Her nose dusted with flour, Maddy said, "We really should think about having our own pastry boxes printed online with our business name on them. It's a great way to show off what we make."

I couldn't believe she was bringing that up again! We'd already been through it, and nothing had changed since yesterday. I tried to keep my voice steady as I said, "Hey, maybe we shouldn't worry about packaging right now. Let's just focus on having enough treats made for the marathon."

Maddy didn't respond, but I noticed that she started working more quickly—and sloppily. The faster Maddy worked at tracing circles for *macarons*, the sloppier her circles looked.

"Maddy, slow down!" I said. "French treats should be beautiful."

"Are you saying I'm doing a bad job?" she asked, looking up from her work.

The Delivery

"No, but . . . you're working so fast that sometimes things come out a little less than perfect, if you know what I mean."

"Maybe *you're* being too picky," she said, her eyes flashing.

"Maybe I'm picky because we *need* to be," I retorted. Words were flying fast now.

"*We?* Are you sure it's really *our* business?" Maddy asked, her eyes half closed like a green-eyed cat. "Or is it *yours?*"

Her words hung there for just a moment, and then she whipped off her apron, which got tangled in her thick red hair. She finally wrestled the straps free, and then threw the apron on the counter. "You can have your perfectly picky *pâtisserie,* Grace," she said. "I quit!"

Maddy yanked open the screen door, stormed outside into a lightly falling rain, and left.

Ella and I stared at the closed door for what seemed like an hour.

Finally, Ella turned to me, her eyes wet with tears. "Do you think she means it?" Ella whispered.

My shoulders rose in question. I couldn't believe what had just happened.

"Girls?" Mom called from the living room. "Everything okay out there?"

I called back and fibbed. "Yeah, we're fine!"

I wasn't ready to have Mom come in and try to patch things up for us. If she did, I knew I'd break into tears. And right now, I needed to be angry so that I could keep going. If I let myself start crying, I wouldn't get anything done today!

"How can she just walk out on us?" I whispered. I stared again at the closed door, hoping Maddy would show up again at any minute.

Ella just shook her head.

For the next few hours, Ella and I worked at finishing dozens of *macarons* in a rainbow of colors—mint green, pale blue, and soft yellow—all lined up in pretty rows by color on the counter, just like at a French *pâtisserie*.

As they cooled, I snapped a photo.

Click!

I wanted to feel happy and proud about how beautiful they looked, but instead I felt depressed. Without Maddy, our business felt like a deflated party balloon.

Before going to bed that night, I e-mailed off a

photo of the *macarons* to Sylvie. *Aimes-tu mes macarons?* I asked. "Do you like my *macarons*?"

But what I really wanted to ask my cousin and con-sultant was this: *What do you do when your bakers—and co–business owners, and best friends—aren't getting along?*

On Monday morning, Ella and I hoped Maddy would show up. We waited for half an hour, but . . . no Maddy. I tried to think of something that would make us feel better.

"Hey, Mom, can we check our website?" I called to her, sliding into the computer chair. Ella and I had been so focused on making treats for the marathon—and on the fight with Maddy—that we hadn't checked it since delivering pamphlets a couple of days ago.

Mom hovered nearby to answer any questions that came up as we checked for orders. Then—feeling very formal and very grown-up—I typed the password into the administrator's portion of the site.

"Oh, wow. We have an order!" Ella said.

"Oh my gosh!" I exclaimed.

"What do you know, girls," Mom said. "Isn't that fun?"

As we stared at the website, another order popped up right before our eyes.

This time, it started to sink in. We hopped up, cheered, and danced around the kitchen.

"Woo-hoo!"

"Customers!"

Then we sat back at the computer, Ella and I sharing a chair.

In the comments section, a few words of praise for our business showed up, too:

Product	Quantity	Color/Flavor
Macarons	6	Pink

Comment: *So proud of you girls!*

And . . .

Product	Quantity	Color/Flavor
Tartelettes	4	Strawberry

Comment: *I've been waiting for a pâtisserie in Bentwick. I look forward to trying your tartelettes.*

Both orders were from people we knew: Mrs. Crabb and Mr. Williams, who lived in Maddy's neighborhood. When I saw those names, I was excited and sad all at the same time. "Maddy should be here," I said quietly.

Ella nodded sadly. "I know. It doesn't feel right to celebrate without her."

"Let's text her with the good news," I said. I dashed off a text on my cell phone, and then set it beside me, checking it every few seconds. Maddy usually replied immediately. But after ten minutes, there was still no answer.

"Well," I said to Ella, "I guess we have some orders to fill."

We pulled some *macarons* and *tartelette* shells out of the freezer and started to fill the *tartelettes* with fresh strawberries. But that's when it hit me—we didn't have any packaging for them! We needed to make a mad dash to the Kitchen Shop. We didn't have a choice now—there was no time for online ordering.

"Business picking up?" Mr. Hammond asked as Ella and I rushed in a half hour later.

"Yes!" Ella and I both replied, out of breath.

We went immediately to the packaging section, and

for just a moment I was glad that Maddy wasn't with us. I didn't want to admit that she'd been right earlier: Packaging *was* important. At least Ella and I had no trouble agreeing on what to buy.

We chose the pretty pink boxes that were on sale—and much less expensive than the thicker white ones with the plastic windows on top. Ella didn't have any money, and I had a lot less money to work with now that I didn't have Maddy here to pool money with me.

But the boxes looked sturdy enough, and very professional. I couldn't wait to tuck our *macarons* and *tartelettes* inside!

When Ella and I had our products ready to deliver, we called Mrs. Crabb and Mr. Williams to make sure they were both home for our deliveries. They were. But as soon as we hung up the phone, we ran into our next hurdle.

"I don't think these will fit in my bike basket," said Ella, examining the boxes.

I sized them up, too. "You're right," I said, my shoulders slumping. "They won't fit in my basket either."

Mom overheard us and came in from the living room. "Do you want me to drive you, girls?" she asked. "At least this first time?"

I thought about that. It was a tempting offer. But I could tell by the look on Ella's face that she felt the same way I did: We had to find a way to deliver these ourselves. There *had* to be another solution.

As we walked into the garage to examine our baskets, I nearly tripped over something that I had abandoned by my bike: the bike trailer that Bonbon wouldn't stay in. "That's it!" I said to Ella. "We might as well use my birthday present for *something*."

And that was how we ended up biking to Mrs. Crabb's house with a bike trailer full of French treats. I smiled as I followed Ella along the towpath, feeling proud once again of the way Ella and I had kept going until we'd found a creative solution.

Mrs. Crabb—a tiny woman with a stooped back and silver hair—barely opened her door to peek through the crack.

"Oh, there you are, girls," she said in a wobbly voice as she opened the door wide. "I just placed the order yesterday, and look: Here you are!"

After we handed her the pink box of *macarons*, she invited us to join her on her front porch for a little while. She brought out a pitcher of iced tea and served up a few of the *macarons* on pink glass plates.

"Delicious!" she said, after taking a bite.

I lifted my own *macaron* and then shot Ella a questioning glance. It felt funny to be eating our own products, especially ones that we had just sold to someone else. But Mrs. Crabb seemed grateful for the company. She proceeded to tell us all about her family's history and how one of her great-great-somethings had actually worked at the Slater Mill in Pawtucket, Rhode Island, just over the state line.

Of course, I already knew a lot about the Slater Mill from Grandpa's stories. It was part of how Blackstone Valley came to be called "the birthplace of the American Industrial Revolution." But I didn't want to be rude, so I listened to Mrs. Crabb tell us about the water-powered mill, and about the canals, and then about the railroad that followed.

When we left nearly an hour later, all I could think about was how much time we had spent there—and about how Mr. Williams was probably waiting for us. But when Mrs. Crabb finally waved good-bye, her ear-to-ear smile was a pretty sweet reward.

The Williamses lived just a few blocks away. I rang the doorbell while Ella waited beside me on the porch, proudly holding the pink paper box with four strawberry *tartelettes* tucked inside.

Mr. Williams, in a striped shirt and khaki pants, met us at the door. "Hello, girls. That was prompt," he said, reaching for the pink box.

We handed him his order, and he dug in his shirt pocket and pulled out a check. It was made out to *"La Petite Pâtisserie."*

"Oh," I said, staring at the check. "But, um . . . we don't have a bank account yet."

"Then I guess you'd better start one, hadn't you?" Mr. Williams said curtly. "You girls have a nice day now." And before we knew it, the door was closed.

Ella and I stared at each other for a moment. "What, no iced-tea party on the porch?" I whispered.

Ella giggled. Then we raced each other back to my house. With the empty bike trailer behind me and our first payments in my pocket, I felt as if I were flying.

Broken to Pieces
Chapter 11

*T*uesday morning, Maddy still hadn't answered my text. I guessed she wasn't going to come back to the business, at least not any time soon.

To make things worse, we received our first complaint. Mr. Williams had sent an e-mail:

I am very, very disappointed in your tartelettes. I waited to serve them to friends last evening and when I opened the box, the tartelettes were broken to pieces. A disaster! I could not serve them.

My heart sank. "What do you think happened?" I said to Ella.

"Maybe the box wasn't sturdy enough?" she suggested. Ella looked suddenly droopy, like a stuffed animal with the stuffing knocked out of her.

"Oh, no—I'll bet I wasn't careful enough with the bike trailer," I realized suddenly. "We went over lots of bumps on the towpath, but I didn't think that the *tartelettes* would break apart."

I wanted to blame somebody, but how could I? I'd been the one to suggest using the bike trailer.

Mom wrapped her arm around my shoulders. "Mistakes are going to happen, Grace," she said. "The trick is to figure out how to make it right with your customers, and then learn from the mistake so that you can keep it from happening again."

I nodded sadly.

After Mom went back into the living room to work on lesson plans, Ella and I slumped down together at the kitchen table.

"Maybe we do need stronger packaging," I said.

"But what about Mr. Williams?" Ella asked. "How can we make things right with him?"

I sighed. I wasn't crazy about the idea of going to see him again if he was upset with us, but I knew what we had to do. "I think we should e-mail him to say that we'll deliver another batch of perfect *tartelettes* for free—today," I said.

Ella nodded. Then she blurted out, "Oh, I really don't feel good."

"I don't either," I said. "I'm sad and frustrated all at the same time."

"No, I don't mean it that way," Ella said quickly. "I mean, I haven't felt well since I got here, and now I feel—"

She jumped up and hurried off to the bathroom just off the kitchen. Was she really sick?

When she returned, she said in a wobbly voice, "I need to call for a ride home."

Oh, poor Ella! After her dad picked her up, I felt bad for her, and a little bad for me, too.

Could this day get any worse? I wondered.

"Josh," I said, trying to make myself heard over his piano playing. "Will you come with me? I need some courage, and Ella's sick, and Maddy's not . . . not around right now."

"What's going on?" he asked, looking up from the keys.

"I had a customer complaint," I confessed. "Mr. Williams agreed to try another batch, but he still wants his money back. I need to deliver the *tartelettes*, and this time without breaking them along the way."

"Sure," Josh agreed.

With four new *tartelettes* extra-well padded and packaged, I biked the small order over in the bike trailer, taking a route through town this time instead of the bumpy towpath.

When we arrived at Mr. Williams's house, I opened the box to be sure the *tartelettes* were still intact, and breathed a sigh of relief.

New rule, I told myself. *Check all orders before delivering them.*

Josh waited for me by our bikes as I started down the sidewalk. "You can do this," he called over my shoulder.

"Thanks," I said. I climbed the steps, paused in front of the doorbell for the second time, and then forced my finger forward.

Ding-ding-ding!

When the door opened, I was ready. I didn't even

wait for Mr. Williams to speak.

"I'm sorry the first batch broke," I said quickly. "This one is free." I handed him his check back, along with the box of *tartelettes*. "I hope you'll try us again, Mr. Williams."

He didn't say anything, but he nodded his head at me. As he closed the door, I saw the faintest smile cross his lips.

Would he ever order from us again? I had no idea. But at least I'd done what I could do to make things right.

I set my shoulders and started back down the sidewalk toward Josh.

The next day, I tried to keep working in the kitchen—I really did. I made a few *tartelette* shells so that I could bake and freeze them ahead of time. We could fill them with fresh fruit just before the marathon.

Dad had taken the day off, and he and Josh were working on the bakery cart in the garage. But even with the sound of the saw just beyond the kitchen door, I still felt so alone.

And overwhelmed.

And unsure.

What if it was my fault that Maddy left? And did Ella get sick because she gets upset when the people around her are unhappy?

Then I had to wonder . . . had I pushed my friends too hard because I wanted this business so badly? Had I pushed the fun right out of our time together?

As if in answer, raindrops started pinging against the windowpane.

The more my thoughts clogged with doubt, the slower I worked. Pretty soon I felt as if I were pushing rocks in a wheelbarrow that would barely move.

"Hey, honey," Mom said, passing through the kitchen in her old jeans and a long-sleeved paint-speckled T-shirt. I recognized that as her welding outfit.

"I'm heading out to help Dad and Josh with that cart—to get it started, anyway," Mom said. "I'd invite you to join us, but you look pretty busy."

I nodded.

"What happened to your friends?"

I bit back tears and shrugged.

"You okay?"

I nodded again and tried to focus on working a lump of dough into a *tartelette* pan.

Mom paused and then kissed the top of my head. "I'm proud of you, Grace," she said. "You're doing a *really* good job. I know it's hard work."

"Thanks, Mom," I managed.

"Okay, then," she said. "Promise you won't use the oven without calling one of us in?"

I promised, and Mom finally left the kitchen.

As soon as she was gone, I put the dough back in the refrigerator, washed my hands, and sat down by Bonbon's crate.

Mom said I was doing a good job, but it sure didn't feel that way. I suddenly felt so tired. I didn't have the energy to bake today.

Bonbon started whining softly.

"I know just how you feel, *ma petite chienne*," I said, opening the door of her crate to let her out.

Bonbon trotted after me as I stepped into the living room to grab a throw from the couch. Then I went straight to the place where I always go when I need to turn inward for a while: the cozy bay window seat.

Bonbon followed me there, too, so I picked her up and set her in the window.

I climbed up onto the red-and-white checked cushion, curled on my side into a half shell, and—as Bonbon snuggled against my tummy—pulled the throw over us. Then I turned to gaze out the window.

I watched a single droplet of water find its way down the windowpane. When it hit bottom, I started over, tracing the pathway of another droplet with my finger.

You'd think water droplets would fall straight, but they never do. They travel a little to the left, a little to the right, around a particle of mud or dust here, around a bug splat there, but continuing on . . . just like the Blackstone River.

I could almost hear Grandpa say, "The Blackstone is the hardest-working river in America." It navigates lots of obstacles along the way, but keeps on flowing until it reaches its destination.

I felt a little bit like that droplet, trying to find my way around all sorts of obstacles. But would I ever reach my goal? Would this business ever work?

I just didn't know. I leaned forward and closed my eyes, resting my head against the cool windowpane.

A Playdate
Chapter 12

I don't know how a person can run so many miles without collapsing, but somehow my mom was doing it.

She had woken me up this Saturday morning at seven o'clock, which was later than Bonbon usually let me sleep. Mom had already walked Bonbon so that I could bike with her while she ran. "I think it'll do us both good," she had said.

Now that we were on the trail, with occasional raindrops splattering on my arms and thighs, I was wide awake. I couldn't believe the half marathon was only a week away—and Ella and I hadn't met up to bake since Tuesday!

She had been sick all week, and I'd been too *heart-*sick to bake without her and Maddy. Finally, Ella was coming over today to start our baking back up, but we had *so* much to do if we were going to be ready for our first big sale.

Mom's arms and legs pumped a steady rhythm beside me. Her long runs of eleven or twelve miles were behind her now. This week, she was coasting with shorter and shorter runs to conserve her energy as the half marathon drew close.

I glanced at Mom. Despite her red face and the river of sweat running down her tank top, she looked *happy*. She'd dreamed of running a half marathon and was working every day at making it come true.

"You know, Mom," I said out loud, "sometimes starting a business feels like training for a marathon, too. And lately, without Maddy, it feels like it's been all uphill."

Mom gave me a sympathetic smile. "I'm sorry, honey," she said, in between breaths.

"Nothing's going right," I said. "Maddy's mad at me, Ella's been sick—even Bonbon seems unhappy. No one's having any fun anymore."

"No?" said Mom, glancing sideways at me. "When was the last time you remember having fun?"

I had to think long and hard about that. There was

the sleepover in the tent after the flour incident. But before that? My mind had to go all the way back to France, when I was baking in the *pâtisserie* with Sylvie and Colette.

I suddenly flashed on little Bonbon, too, the first time I saw her in Paris—playing with another dog in the park, her rump in the air.

Poor Bonbon. She was used to roaming free all over Paris, and now she was stuck in a crate so much of the time and could only play with other dogs when she escaped from our kitchen. No wonder she was so unhappy!

A thought started taking shape at the back of my brain, but before it became crystal clear, the raindrops on our heads started coming down stronger. As the sky let loose with a downpour, Mom looked at me, her mouth wide open. Then we both started shrieking and laughing as we raced down the path toward home.

Mom raised her chin, stretched out her gait, and put on more speed, her calf muscles pumping. She sprinted beside me all the way to the Cross Road Bridge, where the rain finally lightened and Mom could slow down to a cooldown pace.

∾ A Playdate ∾

"That's what I call an *instant* cooldown," Mom joked, wringing out her wet hair.

"That's what I call *fun*," I said, catching my breath. And with that one word, answers to my problems popped up like popcorn. I suddenly knew what I needed to do.

"Mom," I said as I hopped off my bike to walk beside her, "I need to give Bonbon more playdates. Maybe I can bring her with me to Ella's so that she can play with Murphy. Or maybe we could close up the gaps in the stone wall around our backyard so that Zulu can come over and play! Can we?"

Mom laughed and nodded. "I think we could, Grace—your dad has been meaning to do that for a while now anyway."

Then another thought struck. "It's weird, Mom," I said. "I've been thinking about how maybe Bonbon and Maddy have a lot in common."

"Oh?" said Mom. "How's that?"

"I think they both need their freedom," I explained. "Bonbon was used to roaming free all over Paris, so getting used to a leash is tough for her. And Maddy, she's a free spirit. If she feels too scheduled or fenced in, she wants to run off—just like Bonbon."

I paused for a moment and then added, "I think that's why Maddy quit. I mean, I like running with an idea, too, but I also like to make plans sometimes. It's like Maddy and I want the same things, but we have two *really* different ways of going about it."

"Like you and Josh?" Mom pointed out. "You're both creative and smart, but you're very different people, too."

"Yeah," I said. "I actually like to find a path through my room."

Mom laughed.

As we neared home, I felt a little lighter. I knew how to give Bonbon more freedom and fun. But how could I do that with Maddy? And even if I could, would she give me a second chance?

From the garage came the whirring sounds of an electric saw and the pounding and tapping of a hammer and nails.

"Come in and see what we've been up to," Mom

prompted me at the garage door.

I couldn't wait to see what kind of progress my family had made!

"You look like a drowned rat," Josh said as I stepped inside the garage.

"You look like you need a shower," I replied with a smile.

"Morning, Grace," Dad said, shutting off his saw and raising his safety glasses. "Your mom was busy last night out here, so we guys decided we'd better hit it hard today."

In the center of the garage stood the simple metal frame of a cart. Around it lay wheels, boards, drawers, handles, paint cans, and different trims.

This was it? I tried not to show my disappointment. How could my family possibly pull this whole thing together before next weekend?

"I know," Mom said. "It sure doesn't look like much now. But that's usually how projects go. You work and work and it doesn't seem like it's going anywhere, and then right toward the end, it seems to all come together."

I hope that's true, I told myself, thinking of all the

baking that Ella and I still had to do. But I was determined to get it done, and I knew that Mom, Dad, and Josh were, too. I had to let them do their thing, while I focused on doing mine.

"I trust you, guys," I said, trying to sound positive. "I know the cart's going to be amazing!"

"Just like your business will be one day soon," said Dad. "Now go forth and bake!" he added cheerily, lowering his safety glasses over his eyes.

I giggled and stepped inside the house after Mom.

When Ella got dropped off later and started tying on her apron, I said, "Do you think we could bake at your house today?"

Ella shrugged. "I'll check, but I'm guessing it's fine. Why, what's up?"

I reached down to scratch Bonbon's head. "She needs more playtime," I said. "I thought maybe she could play with Murphy in your backyard while we bake."

Ella smiled. "I think Murphy would like that, too,"

she said. "I'll have to call Dad first, though, to make sure the chickens are all locked up before we get there!"

We packed supplies for making *truffles* and put them in my bike trailer.

I let Ella ride my bike, and then I followed behind her, walking Bonbon. It would take a lot longer this way, but I knew I couldn't get Bonbon into that trailer.

"Think they'll have the cart ready for the half marathon?" Ella asked as a painted turtle slid off a log into the shallow water of the canal.

"I hope so," I said. "All we can do is try to make enough treats by then. It sure would help if Maddy was with us."

"I know. It doesn't feel right without her," Ella agreed.

The Petronias' backyard was enclosed by a tall wooden fence. At the swing set, Ella's three brothers— Ernie, Eddy, and Eino—were having fun. But I could never tell them apart. They all had curly dark hair and big brown eyes. One slid down the slide, another stood on the tire swing, and the third dug a hole in the sandbox.

When Murphy spotted us, he bounded over, barking.

Instantly, Bonbon wagged her tail. I unleashed her, and off the two dogs went, romping and running around the yard.

The Petronias' toolshed was now the chicken coop, and in a screened run just outside it, a half-dozen red chickens scratched around in the dirt.

"There they are," Ella said proudly. "We already have eggs in the kitchen from them. C'mon, follow me."

Mr. Petronia greeted us at the back door. "The kitchen's cleaned up and ready, girls," he said with a smile. "Have at it, but be sure to call me if you're about to do anything dangerous." He winked, tucked his tablet under his arm, and then headed toward an Adirondack chair near the swing set.

As we pulled out our supplies for "Chocolate Kiss *Truffles*" and set them on Ella's green-tiled counter, I kept glancing out the kitchen window. A few times I caught Bonbon yipping outside the chicken coop, head to her paws, rump up, tail wagging. But when the chickens didn't seem interested in playing, Bonbon left and bounded back toward Murphy. My little dog was having a blast, just as I'd hoped she would.

Ella and I whipped up a mixture in the microwave that included melted white and dark chocolate, warm cream, grated orange peel, and orange extract. Before we could shape the *truffles* into balls, the ingredients needed to cool, so we set the bowls in the refrigerator.

"Let's check our website while we wait," Ella suggested. "We can use my dad's tablet." She motioned me to follow her outside.

Bonbon lapped water from a huge metal bowl and then flopped in the grass beside Murphy.

"You've been playing hard, haven't you, girl?" I said.

Bonbon's tail thumped up and down, but she wasn't about to get up.

When Ella told her dad what we wanted to do, he handed the tablet to us. We typed in our website and the administrator's password.

There weren't any new orders, but there *was* a customer comment on our website.

"From Mr. Williams," Mr. Petronia said, looking over our shoulders.

"Uh-oh," said Ella.

I held my breath as Ella read his comment aloud.
But to my relief—and astonishment—he had written:

*I am very impressed with La Petite Pâtisserie. Though my first
order arrived broken, the girls replaced the broken tartelettes
for free—and quickly. I'm very happy with how they handled
this mistake. I will order from them again in the future.*

"Grace," Ella said, "your idea for making things better with him worked!"

I nodded, and couldn't help smiling. "Yeah, my
mom always says that mistakes are actually learning
opportunities. I guess we learned something from
Mr. Williams. I'm really surprised, though. When I
dropped off the new *tartelettes*, I wasn't sure he'd ever
want to do business with us again."

Ella shrugged. "Well, looks like you changed
his mind," she said happily. "I wish all my mistakes
turned out that well."

"Me, too," I murmured, thinking about the many
things I'd done wrong while starting this business.
And that led me back to Maddy.

Mr. Williams is giving us another chance, I thought.

A Playdate

I wonder if Maddy would, too.

A hopeful feeling swept through me. "Ella," I said, grabbing her hand, "let's go see Maddy. Maybe if I apologize, she'll change her mind about the business."

A big smile broke out on Ella's face. "Let's try," she said, squeezing my hand. "I'll see if Dad can watch the dogs."

She jogged over to her dad, who was pushing one of the triplets on the tire swing. The little boy laughed and squealed. "Higher!" he shouted. "Higher!"

I knew just how he felt. We were on our way to see Maddy, and I was feeling hopeful again. I wanted to reach out my hands and touch the sky.

Everything about the Eatons' white Victorian house seemed tidy. The shrubs were trimmed evenly at the foot of the steps. The white wicker furniture was spotlessly clean.

We rang the doorbell.

When Mr. Eaton opened the door, Maddy stood well behind him, still in pajamas, her hair in need of a brushing and her fingertips darkened with ink.

"Hi, girls," Mr. Eaton said, leaving us alone with Maddy.

"Hi," she said, stepping closer. "I peeked out the window. When I saw it was you, I almost asked my dad *not* to open the door."

I swallowed hard. "I wanted to come over and apologize."

Maddy looked from me to Ella and back again.

"I'm really, really sorry if I hurt your feelings," I said.

"Whatever. It's okay," she said, her cheeks flushing, but I pressed on.

"Actually, Maddy, it's *not* okay. I was so serious about turning what I love into a business that I think I took the fun out of it for you—and for Ella, too. I'm sorry, because we're friends, and we need to go back to having fun again together. It can't all feel like work. Forgive me?"

She nodded. "Yes."

"Start over?" I asked.

"Definitely."

"Then," I asked, "um, want to come over to Ella's

house? We're going to shape batter into balls—"

Ella added, "—and dip them in chocolate—"

"—and then," I said in a whisper, "drizzle chocolate over them."

Maddy looked at us sideways. "Um, *yum.* That sounds like fun. But let me show you something first." She waved us inside.

In the den, the big desk was covered with paper, just as it had been the last time we were there. Maddy reached for a piece of paper and held it up. It had the words *"La Petite Pâtisserie"* printed in an elegant font and an image below of a familiar-looking little dog with a polka-dot bow. *Bonbon.*

"What do you think of this for our logo?" Maddy asked hesitantly. "A French bulldog for a French business? We could put it on our pamphlets and on our website."

"Oh, Maddy! It's perfect!" I gave her a huge hug.

"What a great idea!" added Ella.

Maddy glanced downward as she said, "Well, having something French was Grace's idea, really." She looked back up at me and said, "It was a good idea, Grace."

That made me smile wide.

"So, is that a yes?" Maddy asked us. "You approve of the design?"

"Yes!" Ella and I said together.

"Good!" said Maddy, her green eyes dancing, "because there's more." She reached for something from the printer: a sheet of stickers. At the top of each was the name of our business and the Bonbon logo. Below was our website address and a list of ingredients.

"I thought we could use these stickers on our packaging," said Maddy, talking faster now. "It's way cheaper than buying boxes printed with our logo online, because we can print them ourselves—and make plenty of them for the half marathon!"

I stared at the sticker sheet, shaking my head. "This is such a good idea, Maddy!"

She blushed a little and said, "Thanks. I'm sorry I didn't think of it sooner instead of pushing for buying that expensive online stuff."

"Me, too," I said quickly. "I'm sorry, too. Because you're really good at this creative stuff. I should have let you have fun with it instead of . . ."

"What?" teased Maddy. "Instead of having me

try to draw perfect circles?"

We all cracked up at that. "I'll draw the circles from now on," I said, "as long as you keep making these amazing advertisements. Agreed?"

Maddy gave me a fist bump. "Agreed."

"Wait, let me get in on that!" whined Ella, raising her fist.

I could tell she was feeling a lot better now, too. If Maddy had great *art* skills, Ella had great *people* skills— and she was happiest when all of her people were happy, too.

"So here's what I've been thinking about . . ." I said as Maddy, Ella, and I stood in Ella's kitchen, shaping chilled batter into round *truffles*.

A flicker of worry passed over Maddy's face, so I hurriedly explained. "I've been thinking that the more we each get to do the parts of the baking business that we like, the more fun we'll all have. Maddy, you love getting the word out—and you're amazingly creative and good at it."

Maddy's face relaxed into a smile.

"I love baking, which is pretty obvious," I went on, "and Ella, you're a rock star with numbers but also with people––with our customers. If we turn one another loose in those roles, we might have way more fun and also have a great business. What do you think?"

With her palms, Maddy rolled another ball and placed it on a cookie sheet. "It makes sense to me. If we keep it fun, then even when we have lots of orders to fill, it might still feel like play together."

"I like it, too," said Ella.

I breathed a sigh of relief. Finally, finally, we were getting somewhere. It had been a bumpy road, but I had learned a lot—and I was excited about the ride ahead!

Before our day ended in Ella's kitchen, Ella's dad snapped a photo of us smiling and wearing our aprons—proof that we were actually having fun again while we worked together.

Click!

And then it was time to go home. The thought of walking Bonbon all the way home seemed like a lot of work now, and if Bonbon could have talked, I thought

she would have agreed. She was curled up at my feet
taking a puppy nap after a full day of play with Murphy.

Then I remembered that I had my bike here at
Ella's—along with the bike trailer. Would I be able to
get Bonbon inside for a change?

When I looked at my tired pup, I felt another surge
of hope. Maybe today, things would be different.

I said good-bye to my friends and scooped Bonbon
up into my arms. She opened her sleepy eyes, but didn't
protest.

Then I walked out to the bike trailer as if we had
done it a hundred times before. I unzipped the trailer
and set Bonbon down for a moment while I made a
nice cozy bed in the trailer with my sweatshirt. Then,
calm and cool as can be, I lifted Bonbon and tucked
her into the cozy bed inside. I zipped up the trailer and
hopped onto my bike.

I heard the hint of a whine as we rolled slowly
down Ella's driveway, but I didn't hear any scratching
of paws on vinyl. And when I stopped at the first stop
sign and stepped off my bike to peek into the trailer, all
I could see were two sweet, sleepy black eyes peering
out at me.

Bonbon was too tired to fight me. She didn't seem to mind the trailer tonight. Maybe, in time, she would even start to think it was kind of *fun*.

The Finish Line

Chapter 13

On Friday, the night before the half marathon, Maddy and Ella slept over. After dinner, Mom, Dad, and Josh invited us into the garage for the unveiling of the bakery cart. We all stood shoulder to shoulder, waiting for Josh to pull the bedsheet from the mysterious cart. I could tell by the smile on his face that he was pretty proud of what they'd accomplished.

"*Voilà!*" Josh said finally, yanking the sheet away.

My hand rose to my mouth.

Maddy shrieked, "Oh my gosh!"

Ella started clapping.

I couldn't believe it. "It's beautiful!" I cried, walking around and examining the bakery cart from top to bottom.

It was practical: a rolling cart with two shelves. But it was much more than that. At the top, metal rods

curved into the shape of a heart. Even the wheel hubs
were heart-shaped. Above the glass serving counter
hung a sweet little bell on one side, and a chalkboard
on the other. A display case curved off one side of the
counter, and below was another big shelf for even more
baked goods.

Then I thought about our disaster with the *tartelettes*
that I first delivered to Mr. Williams. "Glass shelves?" I
worried aloud. "What if we break them?"

Josh thumped the glass countertop. "Plexiglas," he
said.

Dad laughed. "We started with wood panels, but it
looked pretty clunky."

"And heavy," Josh added.

"So we started over," Dad said. "And with your
mom's help welding . . ."

"Well, the cart sort of took on a life of its own,"
Mom added. "So, do you think it will work? Do you
girls like it?"

I shook my head. "I love, love, *love* it."

The bakery cart was way beyond what I had expected. But I guess when my family combines their
energy and creativity, they're pretty amazing, too.

"It's perfect," Ella said, gently pushing the handle-bar. The cart rolled smoothly back and forth.

"We tried to make it unique," Dad said. "We figured it had to be as special as what you girls are making. You set the bar pretty high."

I gave Dad a huge, tight hug. "Thanks soooo much!"

And then I turned to Josh. "You know, for a big brother," I said with a smile, "you're not half bad. That's why you get a hug, too."

Josh inched backward. "I was worried that might be coming," he said, as if he didn't like to be hugged. But I knew better.

"You're the best!" I said, throwing my arms around his neck.

Out of the corner of my eye, my parents couldn't have looked happier.

When the alarm woke us, we all jumped out of our sleeping bags. We had a big day ahead! Mom left early to get her race bib and warm up for the half marathon. I brought Bonbon out to play a little with Zulu, who was up early, too. Then, as the sun rose over the Black-stone River, Ella, Maddy, and I filled *tartelettes* with fresh blueberries and strawberries and moved the last of our baked goods from the freezer to the cart. And what a cart it was!

We arranged our treats with care, making sure every *"La Petite Pâtisserie"* packaging sticker was face-out on our bags and boxes.

"C'est bien?" I asked. "Is it good?"

"C'est bien!" Ella replied.

"C'est magnifique!" Maddy chimed in. Even she had started to try out a French word or phrase now and then.

I shot her a grateful smile.

When we all agreed that everything looked extra special and beautiful, we pushed the cart out into the world. Dad helped Ella and Maddy roll the cart while I walked Bonbon, our mascot. Josh followed beside us on his bike. Together we sang *"Frère Jacques"* in a round—*all* the way to Bridge Street.

In downtown Bentwick, a crowd had gathered near the decorated start and finish line—an arch filled with colorful balloons. From a platform up above, an announcer played music and gave updates on the run over a loudspeaker. And just a block away, the high school marching band had gathered, all brass and shine.

We found the perfect spot for our cart between the riverside park and the finish line.

"This works for me," I said to Ella and Maddy. "This way I won't miss my mom when she comes across the bridge."

Mom had already started running before we got here, and I was pretty sure she'd be done in about two hours. I squeezed my eyes shut and made a wish that she'd have a good run today. She deserved it!

Before we even got settled, customers began to show up at our cart. At first it was the early crowd, walking over from the nearby coffee shop with paper cups in hand. "Just thought I'd see what you girls are selling," one woman said.

"French treats," I said with a smile. "Would you like to try a sample?"

Dad and Josh walked toward us with Bonbon on a leash, but just as I waved to them, a little girl with a head full of pretty braids pointed at our sign and then at Bonbon. "Look, Mom! It's the same dog as on this sign!"

Then she raced over to Bonbon.

I had to laugh. Bonbon had the power to draw customers and take them away, too! But within a few minutes, the girl and her mom returned, ready to try a treat.

Ella took care of handling money. Our parents had helped us open a checking account, so we could take checks made out to *La Petite Pâtisserie*, or cash. Ella recorded everything in our business book and kept the money in her zippered waist pouch.

Maddy handed out pamphlets and also added them to bags with purchases. "If you like what you try today, please order from our website in the future," she said to each customer.

As the sun climbed higher and heat shimmered above the river, the crowds near the finish line grew dense. Dad hovered nearby, in case we needed anything. He brought us snacks and bottles of water to drink, too.

A hum filled the air, the sound of people watching for their loved ones to come across the bridge before the finish line. And we were part of it, offering something unique and delicious while they waited. People would look at our sign, mouth the words, and then smile at us, often stepping closer to buy a chocolate *truffle* or a few *macarons*.

"*Merci beaucoup!*" I would say, handing them their purchase.

When Mr. Williams stepped up to our cart, I held my breath. He placed an order for his next big dinner party. "Two dozen strawberry *tartelettes*," he said with a formal nod. "I would be grateful if you could deliver them fresh and on the day of the event."

"But of course, *Monsieur* Williams," I said politely.

And with that, he gave me his first true smile.

When cheering erupted nearby, I glanced at the bridge. The first runners were crossing—arms raised high, bodies lean and muscled—and heading toward the street banner declaring:

BENTWICK'S
LAST BLAST OF SUMMER
HALF MARATHON!

I kept working at our bakery cart, but I started keeping an eye on the bridge for Mom, too.

Over the next half hour, crowds of runners continued to cross the bridge, some running solo, others in small packs. Mom was out there somewhere, and I hoped she was okay. I gazed at the blur of legs and arms and heads. And then, to my surprise, I spotted her! Her face was raspberry-red, but her gaze was completely focused on the finish line ahead.

I darted from the cart. "I'll be right back!" I yelled to my friends above the crowd's constant cheering.

"Dad! Josh!" I called, joining them at the curb nearest the bridge. "She's coming!"

And then there she was, running toward us.

"Way to go, Mom!" I added to Dad and Josh's whooping and cheering. I held up Bonbon so that she could see Mom, too.

As Mom passed, giving us all a tired thumbs-up, I felt a wave of pride. She had been training hard. *And I have, too*, I reminded myself. We were both doing what we loved this summer, no matter the obstacles, and we had kept working at it—stride by stride—to get to this day.

The Finish Line

I kissed Bonbon, who was being so calm and good, on the top of her head. "You understand, don't you, girl?"

Mom was lost in a crowd of runners, and when I glanced over at our bakery cart, a small line had formed in front of Ella and Maddy. They needed my help, but first I had to find Mom. I gave Bonbon back to my dad and then worked my way through the dense crowd. I finally reached her.

"Mom!" I said, rising to my tiptoes. I kissed her rosy face on the left and then on the right. "You did it! I'm so proud of you!"

"And I'm proud of you, Grace! Really proud!" Then she glanced in the direction of our booth. "But you'd better run, honey. You have a swarm of customers!"

"That's good!" I said, spinning away. "*C'est bien!*"

Glossary of French Words

Aimes-tu mes macarons? *(em-tew may mah-kah-rohns)*—
Do you like my macarons?

bonjour *(bohn-zhoor)*—hello

C'est bien. *(say byehn)*—It's good; that's good.

C'est magnifique! *(say mah-nyee-feek)*—It's beautiful!
It's magnificent!

C'est parfait. *(say pahr-feh)*—It's perfect.

crêpe *(crep)*—a thin pancake served with a variety
of fillings

éclair *(ay-klehr)*—a long pastry filled with whipped or
sweet cream, often topped with chocolate

Frère Jacques *(freh-ruh zhahk)*—Brother Jacques; a French
lullaby that is often sung as a round

gâteau *(gah-toh)*—a rich cake

gâteau au yahourt *(gah-toh oh yah-oor)*—yogurt cake

grand-mère *(grahn-mehr)*—grandmother

grand-père *(grahn-pehr)*—grandfather

le chat *(luh shah)*—the cat (male)

macaron *(mah-kah-rohn)*—a double-layer round cookie
that comes in all kinds of colors and flavors

madame *(mah-dahm)*—Mrs., ma'am

madeleine *(mahd-len)*—a small rich cake baked in a
shell-shaped mold

Ma petite chienne est très à la mode. *(mah puh-teet shyen ay trehz ah lah mohd)*—My little dog is very fashionable.

merci beaucoup *(mehr-see boh-koo)*—thank you very much

moi aussi *(mwah oh-see)*—me too

Mon chat dort sur mon lit. *(mohn shah dohr syur mohn lee)*—My cat sleeps on my bed.

monsieur *(muh-syuh)*—Mister, sir

oui *(wee)*—yes

pâtisserie *(pah-tee-suh-ree)*—a French bakery that specializes in pastries and desserts

petite chienne *(puh-teet shyen)*—little dog (female)

petite pâtisserie *(puh-teet pah-tee-suh-ree)*—little bakery

tartelette *(tahrl-let)*—a small tart, or open-faced pastry shell filled with fruit or custard

très *(treh)*—very

très à la mode *(trehz ah lah mohd)*—very fashionable

truffle *(troo-fluh)*—a soft chocolate candy covered with cocoa or chopped nuts

Versailles *(vehr-sahy)*—King Louis XIV's main palace; also the French town where it is located

voilà *(vwah-lah)*—here it is, or there it is

About the Author

Mary Casanova is always full of ideas. The author of over 30 books—including *Cécile: Gates of Gold*, *Jess*, *Chrissa*, *Chrissa Stands Strong*, *McKenna*, and *McKenna, Ready to Fly!*—she often travels as far away as Norway, Belize, and France for research.

For *Grace*, she returned to Paris—this time with her grown daughter, Kate—where they biked, explored, and took a French baking class together. Mary comes from a long line of bakers. Her grandmothers baked fragrant breads; her mother made the "world's best" caramel rolls and cinnamon rolls; and Mary, too, loves baking breads, cakes, and cookies.

When she's not writing—or traveling for research or to speak at schools and conferences—she's likely reading a good book, horseback riding in the northwoods of Minnesota, or hiking with her husband and three dogs.